Totally Bound Publishing books by Landra Graf

Bad Boys of Space
A Talent for Trouble
A Gamble Among Sheep
The Body Collector

I0670563

Bad Boys of Space

THE BODY COLLECTOR

LANDRA GRAF

The Body Collector
ISBN # 978-1-83943-913-1
©Copyright Landra Graf 2020
Cover Art by Erin Dameron-Hill ©Copyright September 2020
Interior text design by Claire Siemaszkiewicz
Totally Bound Publishing

THE BODY
COLLECTOR

Dedication

To Lori, Cate and Kat—without you, the books
don't happen.

Chapter One

There were only two things a grown man could depend on in outer space—his personal possessions and his knowledge. For Big Al Smith, these were his ship and his knitting skills. Everything else was fickle, especially people, and he'd learned to ride the current.

Which was how he'd gotten himself covered hip-deep in yarn and working on another sweater. He liked sweaters. In the cold of space, they served as stress relief as much as for keeping bodies warm. Brownish-red was where he always started, rust-colored yarn being the cheapest in most places. It cost next to nothing to drop sheep's wool in Mars mud. Leave it there long enough and the rusty color of the Mars surface could turn anything a mud brown.

"Boss."

The name Al heard the most came rattling down the hallway. Al scrambled upward in his seat, grabbing the whole of the knitting off his lap and dropping it into the bag at his feet. Sure, his crew were well informed about his preferred hobby, but he did his best to keep from advertising it. The stigma around women's work being done by a man still existed in this crazy universe.

"In here, Mangle."

His first mate poked his head into Al's office. The office gave way to his quarters through a separate door, one he tossed his bag of knitting through.

"Working on a new one?" Mangle's question came paired with cynicism.

"Got to keep busy waiting for the next assignment." They'd been docked in Jupiter's main city of Helios for the last four days—service work on the damn slip drive. Al had argued against it, but the BCS, Body Collection Service, ultimately got the final say. He was required to have the drive serviced after so many deployments. The number had been hit twice and he'd refused until they'd forced the issue.

"Speaking of assignments, the service finally assigned us some more help."

Al leaned forward and groaned as he swiped through the holo-screens. "Another one. Didn't we say we were only taking on seasoned professionals from now on?"

"Doesn't seem to matter what we want," Mangle replied, leaning against the doorframe.

Al swiped away the profile. He despised new recruits with a passion. They always had ideas, freethinkers who had no clue what enlistment really meant. He wasn't even as strict as some of the captains. "Hypocrites, all of them."

"Yeah, you are. Also, they sent over the new job. Some dead bootleggers, got caught by APUPS hauling contraband."

Finally, the next job in a list of about twenty Al would need before he could escape. Twenty pickups, less than a row for his sweater. It still seemed like it would take forever at the rate the BCS sent him assignments. "Finally, no more sitting around."

"Less time for you to knit. What do you want me to do with the fresh meat?"

Al sighed. He'd already forgotten about that one. "Work with Frankie and get take-off squared away. Have Duffy or Bertha bring the recruit to me."

He ignored Mangle's comment about his knitting — his second in command had a right to be aggravated. The *Acheron* should have been Mangle's command. It wasn't Al's fault. He'd no choice unless he wanted to give up the pay scale that came with a captain's rank, and that would never happen. *At least not until I can get the hell out of here.*

"Fine, boss. Might I suggest you try to keep this one around? We need a little extra help here. It would stave off suspicions."

Another problem Al would have to deal with someday. He'd made the mistake of involving Mangle in his side business, the only thing keeping him floating now. He'd be damned if he'd allow Mangle to blackmail him the way he'd already been forced into this illegal mess. A new recruit meant them being secretive about their processes. "We'll see."

Let's hope they like brown.

Loyda Miles stared at her short, ragged nails. They were nothing like how she normally kept them. This entire situation was so far from anything she'd done since becoming an investigator for parliament, but she'd had no choice.

Frankie, a female pilot with a shock of red hair, frowned at her. "You're from where?"

"Ganymede." The cover story she'd run with. She prayed it held up.

"Why leave that place?"

"Work dried up. My family worked for Grecia." It should have been enough. News of the death of the only cartel leader living off Earth had spread far and wide throughout the galaxy. Her only trouble was it had been six months. *Take the story.*

"Similar things happened to my parents, why they tried to strike it rich in those mines on Mars. But there's no such thing as getting ahead in this universe. Fairy tales. Why I chose to become a pilot, get the hell off that deadbeat rock."

Loyda had heard similar stories growing up. The idea people that could change their fate working for the BCS, mining on Mars, getting into drug running and bootlegging... so many possibilities, and yet she'd never met a single person who'd been successful. Each venture ended in heartache, and most of the time with some sort of injustice.

"Yeah, but at least here you get a bed and guaranteed food."

Frankie chuckled. "They say a lot of things in the recruitment office."

Yes, but they couldn't tell her what she really needed to know. Who was responsible for all the missing bodies? She'd tracked movements around Callisto and other planets and moons for the last couple months. Her work on the plot to stop mass killing on Callisto had ended successfully, but she'd never caught the person behind the whole thing. The name she'd received didn't make sense, as it tied to an ambassador for parliament, which was impossible. *'Parliament helps the people...'* Her mother's words, recited a multitude of times. Especially anytime Loyda talked about becoming a government investigator instead of signing up for duty as an ambassador.

Regardless of her past and the failures in the investigation, she couldn't let this go. There were still too many bodies unaccounted for, still too many people who had died unnecessarily, and someone needed to be brought to justice. Her boss barely agreed but was giving her one more shot.

Proof... She needed physical evidence of some sort or she'd be reassigned, and her time was short. The only direction that made sense was someone in Body Collection, who had partners and was trying to undermine the government.

Her research had led her to the Acheron and the ship's elusive, hermit-like captain, Alexander Smith.

"What's the captain like?"

Both of Frankie's eyebrows rose. "He's not the sort to get intimate with the help. BCS rules. If you think flirtation will get you extra rations, it won't. Al hates new recruits too."

Loyda's sense never betrayed her and something about Frankie's crossed arms spoke volumes. Most likely the woman saw Loyda as a threat. *And she has no clue how right she is.* "I am here to learn the trade. Not be a sponge."

Frankie laughed. "Wow, they breed 'em naive on Ganymede."

"Who's naive?" Mangle, the first mate, stepped out into the cargo bay area. Loyda had met him first when coming on board. Mangle had a thick bushy mustache — in fact, he had a lot of hair in general — and a wiry build. He reminded her of a furry bush animal that lived around the lake at her childhood home on Saturn.

"The new recruit, who else?" Frankie replied.

"My momma said the same about me." This came from the much larger man who tugged a cloth cap over the top of his head.

Frankie laughed. "Bertha, that's still true. Any other questions, space bait?"

At the same time, Bertha groaned. "Why do you call me by my full name, Frankie? I got a nickname that works just fine."

"We prefer to call you by your full name on this boat. Halt on the questions too. Captain wants to meet the fresh space bait and we have a new assignment. Frankie—"

Mangle's words were cut short as the bay doors clanked and creaked open. The ship was in desperate need of an overhaul. Duffy, the engineer, rolled in on the back of a double-wide hoverbike designed specifically for supply runs but looking as derelict as the ship itself. If this crew was knee-deep in illegal activity and killing of innocents, they weren't getting paid enough, or they were good actors.

"I got everything," Duffy hollered as he brought the bike to a stop, the colorful wheels coming to a halt and bringing an end to the multi-spectrum light show that reflected off the ship's walls.

"Even my pork skins?" Bertha's voice came out more like a yell, since he started talking as the engine died off.

"Yes, even the pork skins, though I couldn't get as many with the amount of crinkle you forked over."

"Those things are nasty." Frankie's upper lip curled and she turned away from the group. "Mangle, let's get this party going—aren't you always saying time is flash?"

Loyda took it all in—Frankie's bad attitude, Bertha and Duffy still debating how many pork skins could be bought with gold leaf and Mangle shaking his head. The crew appeared dysfunctional and nothing like a group of masterminds killing people for bodies.

Mangle cleared his throat, then yelled. "That's enough!"

Frankie came to a halt and the other men froze mid-argument. Loyda did everything she could to keep a straight face. Maybe this whole idea was a crapshoot and she could leave now.

"Duffy, unload. Frankie, you're with me. Bertha, take the recruit to the captain. He wants to meet her."

Too late.

"Let's go, girlie." Hulking Bertha came up beside her and motioned with his arm to follow. Loyda did as told without looking back, hefting her faded green duffel bag onto her shoulder—a borrow from her boss, since her luggage was top of the line.

"I have a name. If you call me by mine, I'll do the same for you, Bert."

Bertha glanced over his shoulder, one eyebrow raised. "Heard that, huh? You stick around longer than a solar week and I'll consider it. But good guess on the nickname."

Well, this could prove more difficult than she'd planned. Maybe her captain had been right, and she should stop chasing dead ends. They entered a stairwell, with stairs leading up and down.

"Is that how you get to the slip drive?"

Bertha gave her a scowl. "I'm not here to give you a ship tour. I am taking you to the captain as asked."

"You always follow orders?"

A laugh echoed around her as Bertha took the stairs up one floor, Loyda following.

"Girlie, when you're floating the currents, following orders keeps you alive."

She sucked in a deep breath and bit back the retort forming on her lips. Following orders was ingrained in her too, but doing the right thing trumped orders every time. Going undercover, she'd failed to think about what would happen if she was asked to break the law. Trailing behind this large man, who appeared to dim the lighting in the corridor they walked down, reminded her that she was completely out of her element. Before, she'd been confident in her choice to infiltrate this ship. Now, not so much.

Chapter Two

Big Al sighed as he heard the voices in the hallway and Bertha's clomping footsteps. *The recruit, damn.* He finished his last loop in the row then stuffed everything back into the knitting bag, and kicked the bag underneath the desk for good measure. He didn't need to give the newest addition any false ideas about him or the type of leader he was. No one needed to think he'd gone *soft*.

The word made his blood boil, as memories bubbled up of the BCS heads coming down on him for allowing his sister to run off with his ship. When he had got *Styx* back, the powers on high had taken it away from him. *Left me stuck, and now shorthanded.*

"Captain, hope you're decent. Got the space ba— erh, newbie here to meet you as ordered."

The door was open, but Bertha had some weird thing with privacy, respecting it. *Uncommon on a ship with a bunch of castaways.*

"Come on in." Al looked up, ready to see a face of someone young, dumb and ugly. Instead he had to keep his jaw clenched tight. The woman who entered in front of Bertha was too petite, too clear-skinned and too luxurious to be on a ship like this. Her clothes were dull, dingy green, her cargo pants sporting a few holes, but, by golly she looked…

"Here we are, girlie. This is Captain—"

"Alexander Smith."

Big Al shook his head, mainly to clear away the daze which that sultry-sounding voice of hers had left him in. "It's Captain to you. Big Al to family and friends, of which you are neither."

"Aye, aye, Sir." She clicked her heels together and stood ramrod straight. Her brown hair wrapped around her shoulder in a long ponytail.

Damn me to the Mars Mines. He was a boss, her superior. *Hypocrite.* Okay, he'd fooled around with Frankie from time to time, but that was different—they'd known each other on Mars. *Grew up together.* Frankie was a safe choice, who wanted a good time and no commitment.

"Your name, recruit?"

She smiled. *Damn her near-perfect teeth and full lips.* "Loyda Miles."

Her name should have been trouble. Her clear skin, clean clothes and new grav boots told her story. She was green, brand-new, with no idea what kind of hard labor and dangerous situations were caused by working on a body barge. *Perfect.*

"Have you been told what your job will be here?"

"No, Captain."

Bertha chuckled.

"Got something to add, Bertha?"

The bulky ship's chef shook his head. "No, but I'll enjoy the show."

"Get your ass to the galley and secure the stores Duffy brought back, and when you're done, tell Duffy to move his crap upstairs."

"Done, Captain." And Bertha left like a wild pack of Mars mongrels was chasing him.

"What is my role on the ship?" Loyda, along with her freshness, possessed a cultured accent as well.

"Whatever we say it is. Skinning, scraping, engineer assistant, janitor...you are the lowest-ranked person aboard this vessel based on your service time. Meaning you've signed up for whatever nasty chores we can assign, of which there are plenty."

She frowned, and Big Al wanted to cheer. He'd keep her on for this run—it'd take them a couple solar days, and by then she'd be begging to transfer to another barge, one willing to play mommy to new collectors who couldn't handle things.

"I thought I was here to learn how to process bodies?"

"Oh, you will. Though work like this sucks away at what soul you have left living in this godforsaken world. Which drives me to ask, why in the hell would you sign up for service?"

Loyda seemed to stand up even straighter. "A job. Steady work, steady pay and regular meals."

Al chuckled. "They're still selling the same lies. You only get that stuff if you're with a barge crew willing to do any job to get the bodies in. It's not pretty work, not easy. Lucky for you, this crew does whatever is needed. What's your background?"

"Did they not send my profile over?"

How naive is she? "Profiles are crap. Anyone can say whatever they want on a profile. I am asking you to skip the bullshit and lay it out straight." Al steepled his hands together, propping them under his chin. He found himself eager to know more about her, where she came from and how the hell she'd survived falling into the natural cynicism that eventually took over everyone in the galaxy.

"Fine. I grew up and worked on Ganymede—my family was employed by Grecia. When he died, we tried to find other work. Unfortunately, we had little luck. So I struck out, but there's nothing unless you're into selling your body, which I won't do. I tried my hand at some hard labor in the sludge pits on the other side of Jupiter, but the money's not as good as what the BCS promises, so here I am. I can handle the rough work, the nasty work, and am not afraid of a scuffle." The woman spoke with conviction, but hell—if she could hold herself in a fight, he would start one just to see it.

"Fair enough. Though we try to refrain from scuffles on board this ship." Al stood up from his chair, straightening his shirt as he went. "Now for the tour. Follow me."

He enjoyed how her eyes widened at the size of him. He wasn't small, nor as tidy as she appeared. No, his shirt had about five patched spots from other shirts and his pants and grav boots had been kept for two years longer than they should have been. But material things were nothing when one was on the journey to retirement.

Al walked out of his office doors and headed back in the direction she'd come. His room and office were at the end of the tech hall. "This house hallway is crew quarters. As you come to the stairs, there's the galley, and the opposite side of the hall is the communal bathroom."

"Which one is mine?" The hopeful voice gave her away. He'd make her regret it.

"None of these. You'll be down in the engineer room quarters. Designed for someone to sleep and play watch in case anything goes wrong." He could picture her grinding her teeth and making obscene gestures at his back. Ones he'd gladly take her up on if she offered. He needed to stop thinking that way.

"Isn't that the engineer's job?"

They had reached the stairwell and, as he took the first step down, he held on to the railing and pivoted to face her. "It is, and he'll help, but you'll be the one to sound the alarm. Duffy has more seniority than you do. Therefore, the role is assigned to the one with the least experience."

Not really, but in this case, he would make an exception, because having her in quarters right down the hall from him would be bad for both of them.

"What if I don't wake up?" She was close enough for him to smell her, and though he could smell her natural odor, there was something sweet underlying it. Which was unexpected and unwanted, since her words inspired him to see her in a bed. *What the hell is wrong with you?*

"Oh, you will. Sweating like you're a mile from the sun or choking on the steam of piss and powder will wake anyone. Let's keep moving." Al continued down the stairs, and he heard Loyda's measured steps behind him.

"Outside of the galley and this storage bay, you'll spend the most time in the body room. Won't bother with that tour until we get some bodies. As for callsigns and coms, this ship is called Acheron. Most of the ships in the fleet are just like this. I used to have a second ship, Styx." He reached the last step and came to a little landing area.

Seconds later Loyda stood beside him, the top of her head about three inches from his shoulder. "What happened to the other one?"

"My sister happened."

Grumpy and vengeful—these were the two words Loyda would use to describe Al in her first report to her boss. The man had issues and was every bit as big as Bertha. Thick build, bright ginger beard, bald head. A contrast of extremes and one she'd never thought she would find attractive until now. She'd always enjoyed her men closer in size to her. But with that came egos, often easily insulted by her desire to be a top investigator, a role typically filled by men.

With Big Al, that wouldn't be the case. No, he was confident, brash, almost rude to her and owned it. She'd met men like that, but normally it was because they dismissed her as a woman. Big Al seemed to want to get rid of her.

"Your sister, who's she?"

Big Al growled. "No one worth talking about."

Add 'doesn't trust easily' to the list. Loyda had heard of his sister, knew a lot about her and had even briefly chatted via holo-vid with the force of nature known as Antonia Morales. She'd married an infamous drug runner, taken down the drug lord Grecia and helped a nightclub owner start his own planet.

Al didn't wait for her. No, he took off down an even narrower hallway. She was surprised he fit, and the light truly got blocked. Right past the engines, she saw him lean through a doorway and flip a switch. He never stepped inside, just motioned to her to come closer.

"This is your home away from home."

She peered around the doorway, silently praying to whatever goddess who chose to hear that her imagination would be proven false. *Wrong.* Inside was *worse* than she'd imagined. "When's the last time new mattresses were purchased?"

"Not in years." Al smashed his meaty hands together, small popping noises filling the air as his knuckles cracked with the force. "We don't have as much work, therefore not enough funds to replace things. We take everything we can get, but supplies have gotten more expensive and we don't always make quotas."

Was it wrong to be attracted to someone who lied about everything? Because she had seen the quota reports. Acheron had made every one for two years running. The crew ran lean, though, which made it easy to get on. No reports explained why, beyond Big Al having been cited for dereliction of duty for allowing his sister to steal one of his ships. That had happened over a year ago and could be the reason for the lack of sign-ups, but she didn't believe that entirely.

"Toilet works, though. Showers you'll have to get upstairs in the communal bathroom. The times are posted, for men and women. We try to respect privacy where we can, within reason."

The toilet compared to prison toilets, with a small pull-out sink. The only bright side was the fact that she would be secluded away from anyone else, freeing her up to make her reports to her boss.

"You'll have to pick up a set of linens from storage." Duffy's voice echoed down the corridor. "Took what was on the bed with me. I like my blanket and pillow."

"Thanks for that," she hollered back. Stepping into her room, she tossed her duffel onto the bed. The frame creaked under the weight. "I don't know if that can hold me."

She looked at Big Al as soon as the words were out and could have sworn she saw a fire behind those eyes, one that inspired her mind to wander in naughty directions, because she imagined they would need a much larger bed. *Get it together, Miles.*

"If it can hold me, it will fit you fine."

A flush of heat crept into her cheeks. He would swallow that bed with his size, and she'd have to climb on top —

"Now we have that settled, let's go over a few basic rules." Al lowered his head slightly and stepped into the room.

Loyda should have felt claustrophobic, but instead the urge to snuggle up close to him had her planting her feet firmly in place. "All ears."

Big Al held up one finger. "One. When we have a job, everyone reports for duty, no matter what time of solar day. Two. My word is the only word, so if I tell you to do something, it supersedes any direction given by someone else. Three. Your earnings are based on the ship's intake and processing. Four. All bodies are worth something."

His gaze trailed up and down her form, and she grew hot under the scrutiny. Then he leaned in closer, his growly voice softer this time. "Including yours, if anything bad happens. So don't let anything bad happen."

Loyda couldn't breathe for a second, could barely register that he was basically warning her she could die. Maybe she should take it as a threat, but the way he stared at her implied he might eat her alive. *Yes, please... What is wrong with me?*

She licked her lips and opened her mouth to respond, when Frankie's voice crackled over the intercom. "Prepare for takeoff."

Chapter Three

The recruit flustered Al, which was exactly why he'd stupidly invaded her space. *More like get her to stop asking questions or making comments.* Since takeoff, he'd seen her visiting with Duffy and Bertha and bothering Mangle for the bedding storage location. He half expected her to start opening every door and storage compartment she came across. Her eager nosiness reminded him of the extra powder he was storing in the air holds. Maybe putting her in the engineer's room had been a bad idea.

Yes, he'd deliberately put her there to get her far away from him. But so far it appeared she'd cause trouble anywhere she went, and by trouble, he meant upheaval. He was not used to having someone untried and lacking in knowledge on his ship.

After seeing her flutter around from his seat on the bridge, he decided to take a breather in his room. Frankie knew to alert him when they arrived at the ship. He'd barely gotten his bag from under his desk when the door burst open.

"If she complains one more time about the state of the ship and the rules around BCS accommodations for crew members, I'll shoot her and process her body on principle." Mangle's mustache twitched and his eyebrows bunched.

"Seems our fresh face is bothering more than one of us. Did you deter her?"

Mangle crossed his arms. "I told her to file a complaint with the service and see how much they really cared. If she still isn't happy, she can transfer. But why the hell did you put her in Duffy's quarters?"

"For the reasons you just provided."

Mangle sighed. "We need help."

"We need to be left to our work." Al didn't want to have to cut another person in on the fees he was receiving. He'd already lost a significant cut by having to dole out some extra to the remaining members of his crew. Another mouth to feed would not get him closer to retirement any faster.

"You're giving this one too much credit in the intelligence section. She'll never notice what we're up to."

This was where Al and his first mate differed. Mangle often underestimated people and situations. Al was always more wary, especially after Toni's betrayal.

"Acheron crew, we have arrived at our destination. Time to go to work." Frankie's voice crackled over the coms.

"We can discuss our opinions and your desire to constantly believe too much in others later. I want everyone suited up, except Frankie."

They marched, Mangle in front of Al, to the cargo bay. Duffy, Bertha and surprisingly Loyda were already present when he arrived.

"Everyone, suits on." Al's announcement got everyone moving toward the suit storage compartments. Inside were all the things a successful body collector needed — space suits, steel-lined grav boots, magnetic pingers, haul lines, water torches and a special explosive called lock magic. "Everyone slide into a rig. Get your boots on and grab a belt. The details are as follows. We have an estimated five bodies. We go in fully suited and ping the bodies with the metal discs in the pouch on your belt. Bertha will take care of the rest."

"For once, I would fatching love it if one of you handled the heavy lifting. Once." Bertha zipped up his suit and snapped his belt in place.

Mangle chuckled. "Yeah, and I'd love three house women in my quarters. We can't all have our dreams come true, and that goes for you, Bertha."

Al cleared his throat and reached for his helmet. "Let's get this wrapped up in the next couple hours. We'll be processing all night."

"Uh…" Loyda stood there, suit half on and her belt at her feet. "I can't."

Loyda had signed up for a lot of things, but not going out in space. Until the age of ten, she'd never left Saturn and had only traveled by mag train to go anywhere. Traveling in space always bugged her because of the millions of things that could go wrong. The million and one ways to die.

Now they wanted her to go out in the very thing that could kill them if their suits got even slightly torn.

"What can't you do?"

Any of this, she wanted to scream. She'd never slipped into a space suit and launched into the cold, dark currents from a ship door. Her space training was limited, based on emergency situations only. Her plan had been to infiltrate the ship and work janitorial or processing. Sure, Big Al had said all hands on deck for every job, but she'd never believed that meant everyone participated in all aspects of the job.

"Loyda, are saying you are unfit to do the work?" Big Al's question sent alarm bells clanging in her head.

She had let her fear get the better of her and voiced it. She'd hunted and captured thieves, kidnappers and a slew of murderous people in her career. She could handle a walk in space, damn it.

If she didn't suck it up and kept letting her fear voice itself, her cover would be blown before she even got started. She needed to toughen the hell up or turn in her investigator license now. And she refused to surrender her career until she had to. It would be her choice, her decision.

Mangle clapped her on the back. "It's cool, recruit. Okay, Duffy. Pay up."

"Shit," Duffy replied.

Big Al raised both hands. "Hold up. Let the woman speak. I want to hear it from her own lips."

Loyda summoned her best smile. *I deserve an acting award.* "Just messing with you jerks. Let's finish up and stake our claim. There's bodies to retrieve."

Mangle stomped off first, a litany of curses streaming from his lips. Duffy just smiled, while their captain looked at her with his eyes narrowed. Under scrutiny, she tried to keep the smile in place while securing her belt and checking the compartments.

Bertha slid his helmet into place, his voice a booming echo. "Miles got a set of nuggets on her, eh, Captain?"

"It's not nice to screw with people," hollered Mangle from across the room.

She pivoted on her foot and yelled back, "Not nice to bet against your crew members either."

Big Al finally took his attention from her without comment and she dropped her act, focusing more on trying to familiarize herself with all the tools on the belt. *Including a weapon...*

"Why do I have a knife?"

Duffy saddled up next to her and started grabbing the various tools and calling them out. "Refresher course, because the initial entry training at the service sucks. You saved me a nice bit of crinkle, so consider this my way of saying thank you."

He grabbed her hand and put it on the knife. "Cutter—in the event a line gets tangled or a body is stuck, use this. Next, the pingers. Magnets we attach to the body. Just stick it to them. If there're no clothes, you'll press a button on the top to release a pin and stick it in their skin."

"But they're dead." Loyda tried to keep the concern from her voice, but somehow the idea of damaging the deceased seemed wrong.

"And they don't feel any pain. Now the haul line with clamps. You'll use this to connect to the tether securing Acheron to our target and you will disengage on successfully landing over there. Do not disengage until your grav boots have officially locked on to the ship surface."

Loyda kept up her inner resolve, though fear battled hardcore against her efforts. "How will I know when they are secure?"

"You'll hear it. And finally, the water torch. This is another tool for getting bodies loose. Sometimes they're melted to metal or parts of the ship. That happens, do not cut the body. Cut the item with the body attached."

"Why?"

A clanging sound sidetracked them both. Big Al, Bertha and Mangle all got closer to the ship door. Loyda's gut churned like a trolling motor, ramping up speed as they all secured helmets. She still needed to put hers on. *They won't open the hatch until we're all ready.*

"Loyda, back at me." Duffy got her attention again with a slap to the shoulder.

She looked at him, almost wishing the guy with the soft brown hair and matching eyes sparked something for her, more than the large-and-in-charge captain did. Duffy seemed nice.

"We cut the ship because if you accidentally cut into bone, we lose some of our profit. Bodies don't get cut on until back on the ship. Preserve it at all costs."

"Are you both planning to work today or what?" Big Al roared. "This door opens in one solar minute."

Fatch. Both she and Duffy scrambled to get their helmets in place. The seal hissed, signaling that she'd done it right. *Small favors.* She would need more luck than that for this run. As Duffy headed for the door, she followed.

The captain's voice came through the helmet sound system crystal clear. "Bertha is out first, followed by Duffy, Mangle, Loyda and me."

She nodded. No other verbal declaration was given by anyone else. The door opened two seconds later, and she heard and felt the click of her grav boots giving the extra gravity that would keep her from being sucked out of the door.

Fearlessly, Bertha hooked up his tether and pushed off from the floor, launching into space. Duffy and Mangle followed with no hesitation. Loyda took a deep breath and made her way to the tether. She grabbed her clasp and line, ready to attach, when Big Al brought a hand over hers.

"Are you confident in your abilities? If not, give up now. I can't risk the lives of others for someone who's trying to overcome a fear of space."

She frowned, part of her wondering if he was saying all this because she was a woman. "I got this, and I'll show you."

Yanking her hand out of his, she secured her clamp to the tether as she pushed off. The rush and cold hit her full force, but it came with a weightlessness she was unaccustomed too. Like a ball soaring across the sky, she reveled in the momentary euphoria, an experience unlike any other.

Big Al followed and came up on her much faster. "You should never look backward, only forward at your destination."

Then he grabbed hold of her belt and hauled her to him. She gasped at the contact, at how right and how briefly arousing it felt to have such strength grasping onto her. "I had it—*oomph!*"

Her eyes closed instinctively and her whole body cried out in brief pain as they encountered the wall of the other ship.

"You all right?"

At first no, but could a body radiate heat in space? Because having him pressed against her was warming up everything, like a priming slip drive. "I am fine."

"Good. Now put your feet flat against the wall to secure the grav and I'll unhook you."

She opened her eyes. They were hanging in space from a tether attached to a ship wall. A glance to her left showed her the ship's doorway, one Bertha had already appeared to torch through, giving the go-ahead signal as he, Duffy and Mangle got inside.

"Loyda. Now."

Her movement thrust her breasts hard against Big Al's chest and he groaned. *Thank goodness this whole arousal isn't one-sided.* The boots clicked and Frankie's voice called out, "Get moving — we have company."

Chapter Four

Just my fatching luck. He'd got Loyda detached from the tether, and he followed suit. All his thoughts about protecting her and the hard-on he was sporting within the confines of his suit evaporated like steaming fuel mix at the thought of losing out on these bodies to some other competitor.

"Duffy, Bertha, are you in?"

"Second lock inside the main hatchway, boss. Bertha is almost through," Mangle replied.

He glanced back at Loyda, who thankfully followed him. She'd been a right fool, but damn if her nuggets hadn't impressed him. She looked like a warrior, fierce and brave, going backwards on the tether. Though she would have been hurt if he hadn't caught up to her. *Let's not forget the feel of her in my arms.*

"Another ship? That's against the rules." Loyda's focus on good faith and honor also hit him in a soft spot.

Duffy laughed. "Boss, less than a solar minute and we're in."

Al reached the first door and extended a hand behind him for Loyda to grab hold of. "Out here there are no rules. Now, let's get those bodies pinged before the bastards have time to get their suits on."

Another glance at Loyda showed him the fearless look in her gaze had been replaced with confusion. A grab and drag brought her between him and Duffy. "Everyone hold tight. Frankie, any clue where they are?"

"On the other side. They shot out a tether. I can't see their launching door, and initial intel showed no entrance from that side."

Shit, they needed to move. Bertha's grunt echoed in his ears as the cook kicked in the door.

"Ping bodies," Al commanded. "Loyda, stay here and as we ping them, guide them out. Make sure they don't get stuck in the doorway. This is precious cargo. Mangle with Bertha, and Duffy with me."

The lights on his helmet automatically came on as he entered. The ship was some sort of asteroid mining venture, from the looks of the crates of rocks against the walls, stacked next to examining tables.

Asteroid mining, what a joke. The idea that asteroids could reveal substances that might prove useful for the future was an ongoing fantasy, one that got people killed. The evidence lay before him. A crew of seven, not five as the service had estimated, lay around the ship's main section. *Caught hauling contraband, yeah right.* Two of them children, buckled into chairs behind a control console. *Damn shame.* While children often suffered the sins of the parents, he'd take their bodies too. *No waste in this damn galaxy.* Al moved there first, cut them free of their harnesses and pinged them.

"Get these two out first, Duffy."

Loyda surprisingly didn't make a sound as the bodies floated toward her in the entrance. Al expected her outrage, to rally at how inhumane and unfair his business was. Toni had said similar things when she'd worked on his ship. For Al, it had become an all-too-familiar sight.

"This is against the rules." Those words again muttered in some outraged puff.

Al stuck another ping chip to another body. "Stuff the rules. Just move fast and keep a steady eye. We may get all this done before our competition gets here."

"How will we keep our merchandise?" Loyda asked.

Al glanced at her and saw she still had a hold on the children. "Let go of them and you'll see. The pingers are specific to our magnet. No other magnet will attract them, just oppose them. A previous engineer worked it up for me."

Everyone had magnet technology with the pinging chips, but Al needed an edge and his sister's engineer, Sampson, had designed them to repel other magnets, giving him a chance to avoid his catch being stolen.

"Bertha, head out."

Bertha nodded and stomped over toward Loyda. He chuckled. "Don't worry, space bait—I'll make sure the payday makes it safely over. You just keep shoveling the bodies out of the door."

"We're almost done."

That was when a muted thud vibrated the ship and part of the wall on the opposite side came off. Al had just pinged the last body, with Duffy shoving it toward the entrance, when four unknown collectors entered through the new hole in the wall.

Mangle merged with the wall behind him, lying in wait. His first mate was really the biggest, sneakiest bastard around. "Mangle, now."

Sneaky, but fast too. In less than five seconds, the first mate had pinged two of the four rogue collectors. The metal discs cutting through their suits and the sudden loss of air pressure rushing through the ship, as well as the rapid departure of the folks in those suits as they headed for the opposite entrance, gave Al time to get into position.

The whole while, Loyda's voice rang out in his ears. "What the hell are you doing? Those are live people!"

"It's us or them, space bait." Mangle's announcement came with a few grunts as the next closest rogue crew member started throwing punches.

Big Al readied his ping gun and pushed off the floor, clicking his boots to free up the gravity. The momentum carried him across the room. *Click, snap,* and his feet were secure on the floor. He held the gun up to the closest one's shield visor and fired.

Another press of the gun aimed at the junction of neck and shoulders ended the fight between Mangle and the remaining member. Mangle shoved the body off him, and at that moment, Al had no sympathy for the poor bastards. He couldn't have any. Sympathy didn't run ships or keep bellies full. He'd learned that on Mars as much as here.

"Duffy, set the dummy."

"Aye, aye." Duffy shoved the dead body toward Loyda and moved over to the entrance the thieving collectors had entered through. He grabbed a small box from his belt, pulled free the antenna at the top, set the firing mechanism, aimed at the ship and fired. The would-be body thieves' ship immediately fritzed, enough small sparks of electricity radiating across the entire hull to send a little light into the ship. Al didn't miss the mistrust on Loyda's face.

He headed for the exit and motioned toward the open hatch. "Head out. All the bodies are on their way. Connect your line and Duffy will draw you back."

"What about the other ship?"

"Let's hope they have emergency beacons."

* * * *

Loyda popped the knuckles on her hands then shook out her arms and shoulders. It took everything within her not to call a halt to this whole plan, and to announce the arrest of Big Al and his entire crew instead. They'd killed people in cold blood, with no provocation—this crew seemed to have issues with probable cause. Stomping on anyone within feet of their claim appeared to be the order of the day. The lawlessness had run rampant and now she'd got stuck taking apart bodies.

The smell itself was bad, but the strain on her joints from hauling things and holding a sprayer down was worse. She brushed against the plugs in her nostrils. No one else wore them. Duffy had snickered when she'd asked for them. *Protocol...* The damn word had made everyone roll their eyes at her. Bertha might have called her a wimp. Mangle had held his hand out to Duffy for another transfer of precious crinkle. She would love to bring the full force of the law down on each one, to prove a point as much as to assuage her pride.

"Oy, bait...we got two bodies left to get into the melter. Hurry up with the wash-off." This from Duffy, who was busying prepping more bodies for said melter.

"They're coming. Not like we're in a hurry." For the last twenty minutes, Mangle had been inside the equipment, rattling around with tools, claiming the damn thing needed work. Despite not being the engineer, like Duffy, Mangle knew a hell of a lot about technical things.

The whole process stank. First, they removed all clothing, shoes and such and threw them into a bin, which Frankie had already rifled through. Next the shaving. She hadn't done that part. No, Bertha wielded the shears on the production line, making each body hairless like a newborn. He talked while he worked too, disturbing shit as if the people were alive and in for regular grooming. Then the lousing. Bacteria grew on people even in space, the cold not being enough to kill them. The lousing powder, some dry concoction, killed bacteria. Then Loyda got the pleasure of rinsing the bodies off.

No tears were shed in this whole process. The bodies of the dead were given no thought or care as they were tossed, turned, mutilated and treated as if they'd never been living. She did her best to think of them as dolls to prevent her eyes from tearing up. The whole act made her less than charitable to her shipmates. No sympathy could be spared for these murderers. At least four bodies that had passed on this belt hadn't deserved death.

Loyda sprayed down the next body, lost in the possibilities. She could arrest them for the murders of the crew, but an argument could be made for self-defense. The Acheron had been assigned to this job. BCS never assigned two ships to the same job, at least not according to the rule book she had read. More proof was needed.

"Melter's ready." Mangle's voice echoed around the room.

She pressed the button on the conveyor belt to move the last body down the line and turned to follow Mangle. His hands appeared mighty full for someone just working with tools to fix a melter. But what did she know? *Nothing.*

The big contraption in the middle of the room provided perfect cover for illegal body-part tampering, what with the noise, the whirling of the exhaust fans and the heating coils as everything fired up. She slid right up next to the far edge, being careful not to come too close. This thing would get hot, no doubt. Peering around the side, she saw Mangle next to Big Al, several big chests at their feet brimming with coolant coils as Mangle removed organs from a wrapped satchel — the dripping blood and the bright reddish-brown color dead giveaways.

Crinkle talks. And people were nothing if not predictable. Harvesting organs from bodies was super illegal, and the black market on Callisto was a prime area to sell and trade for new body parts. In space like this, bodies fell apart quickly. Loyda wasn't ignorant of the fact that Uppers were helping fuel this industry and encouraging collectors to take risks to make obscene amounts of flash.

The lid of the first cooler clanged shut and Loyda took that moment to move toward the sinks. Turning the ion sink on full blast, she let the heated beams remove any trace of bacteria and decay from her gloves. Next came her bare hands. Only then did she remove the nose plugs. *Bad idea.* Loyda gagged. The stench of flesh filled the air. How the hell anyone made it through this whole process without tossing bile made no sense. Her experience with processing was limited to the spot checks and arrests she'd made on other death barges. Knowing how ships were powered had never prepared her for the grim reality.

She stumbled for the door, bracing herself against the entrance to the room and wildly trying to punch in the code to get out.

"What are you doing?" Al's voice sent a fresh rush of panic through her.

She gagged again.

"Shit, Al. Look at her, she's turning green." Mangle's nasally response failed to help, the stench already reaching in deep and wrapping around her stomach like coiled wire.

Heavy footsteps sounded behind her, then the chime of the numbers on the keypad, followed by the *whoosh* of the doors, before a blast of fresh air hit her. She was no longer on her feet, with Big Al's hands grasping her under her armpits like they were still in space, as if she was weightless. He propelled her out of the room, and the doors resealed tight.

When he set her down and turned her to face him, she was unprepared for the concern in his eyes, for that bud of attraction that had been growing since they'd met to reawaken under his gaze. He was a killer. She should want nothing to do with him, and yet...when had someone ever bothered about her?

"Maybe I shouldn't have pushed to have you in the processing room for all this. It's a lot for those who've never done it."

"I—" Loyda coughed, then growled in a futile attempt to clear the lingering stench of flesh from her throat. "Just pulling my weight."

He took a step back. The distance was a good thing, yet she felt the loss. She shouldn't have wanted it or let it bother her, but it remained just the same. "You're looking a bit sick."

"Just need a bathroom break."

Al shook his head. "Take all the time you need, and don't worry about it. We should have prepared you more for the first round of processing—it's not for everyone."

She stared him down, trying to see if he was genuine or not. "Fine. I'll be in my bunk."

She didn't miss the heat that entered his eyes, nor did it help that the look he gave flared something to life in her and brought an instant memory of her body pressed against his, flying through space. Lord, she needed to cool it down, to remind her traitorous physical instincts that the man before her was the enemy.

"See you in the morning. No doubt we'll have a new job then."

She nodded and walked away, attempting to keep her eyes on the path in front of her. There were words she wanted to say, questions she wanted to ask. But none of them took precedence over the most important thing—Al was guilty of murder. And justice would need to be served—by her.

She hustled down the stairs and, once back in her bunk, pulled the communication device out of her pack. A couple of entry codes unlocked it. The device could hack the coms of any ship and keep her presence hidden. She dialed in for her boss's office.

Two tone beeps later, her boss's face flooded the screen. "Miles, report."

"I am stationed on the Acheron with the brother of Antonia Morales, Big Al Smith. We've already completed one body run and the results are what I suspected."

"He's trafficking the drugs?"

"No, he's killed four people in cold blood and is harvesting parts for the black market."

Her boss sighed. "This isn't proof that leads to who is distributing the killer ink you found on Callisto. Who are the four dead?"

Loyda let her shoulders slump. Her boss had been hesitant to send her out, had thought her theories a bit too farfetched, and the burden of proof was always an issue. "The four dead are other collectors. They came upon the Acheron's take and attempted to join in."

"I've heard of collectors trying to steal other assignments, and it's not legal." Her boss seemed less disturbed by this news and more focused on a piece of dirt beneath his fingernail.

"I thought you said murder is murder."

"It is, but our jurisdiction is not the whole of space. That's APUP territory. As investigators we yield such things to their discretion and focus on the bigger issues."

The issue was the cost of life, in Loyda's mind. Who fought for those people? And trying to reconcile her attraction to a man who cared so little—

"The drugs, Loyda...do you have any information on that?"

Not in truth, but... "I know Al has information on the drugs and the bodies. I just need to convince him to talk. If I had permission to bring murder charges—"

"Brass nuggets, woman. You just told me you're a on a ship with killers. What is to say they won't kill you?"

"Nothing." *Therein lies the problem.* The risk was something she thought worth taking. "But you know where I am. If I don't report back within the next eight solar hours, you can guarantee I have been murdered."

"Not sure if I want to take that gamble, but fine. You pick the worst time." Her boss let out a weary groan, which, compounded with the noises of frustration, said something was off. This man had inspired her as a young investigator and it wasn't often that something threw him out of sorts.

"What's happened?"

"The jail on Saturn—it's been attacked."

Whatever nausea and disgust she'd experienced in the body processing chamber came back full force. "Who escaped?"

"That's just it. No one escaped that we know of. The communications officer sent an SOS. Minutes later, we received no response to our hails from the main station on Jupiter. We tapped into the camera feeds and there's no one there. Can't find guards, prisoners, even the main office folks. Everyone disappeared."

It sounded like an eerily familiar story, one she'd seen firsthand on Callisto, where missing persons holo-flyers were plastered on the space station and the number of lost rivaled the living souls. Only one word, one person stood responsible for such chaos—Tuatha.

"Captain, I'll investigate it."

Chapter Five

Al stood back and watched the last body get shoved into the melter. They'd netted far more than planned, even if some innocent lives had been taken. Then Loyda had almost got hurt. They'd been lucky to escape with no major injuries. *Stupid lucky.*

"Don't feel guilty. If we hadn't moved, we would be the ones being shoved into a melter right now," Mangle said, staring him down.

"What guilt? It's worth nothing out here."

Mangle pointed at Al's crossed arms. "Your stance, the frown on your face."

His first mate could believe whatever he wanted, if it threw the fool off the scent of Al's inconvenient attraction toward Loyda. Her looking green earlier, damn close to fainting, had sent his protection instincts into overdrive. He'd wanted to throw her over his shoulder and haul her out of there in some stupid primitive display that would have made him look weak. Instead, he needed to be focused on measuring away those extra four bodies' worth of powder into the barrels he was required to deliver to Tuatha.

Four more pounds closer to freedom. "I'm more frustrated the measurements didn't net out larger. That last one had some larger-than-life bones. Get the extra separated and into the marked barrels. I'm headed to send the report and make arrangements for the drop."

Mangle only nodded in response and moved closer to Duffy, who was hosing down the belts with a cleaning solution. *Dirty business, body processing.* He needed a shower, too. Something to wipe away the human grime clinging to him, the scent of life melted away...*and I need a drink.*

The walk to his quarters was short and sweet, though the shower he took was longer, letting the ion-infused water cycle away the grime. He emerged from the shower and wrapped a towel around himself. The room was cold, but with Al being larger than most, his heft always kept him running a bit hot. The steam kicked up from the water didn't help. A loose towel around his mid-section covered up the important bits, and he enjoyed walking around his quarters and office, air-drying to his heart's content. For being stuck in a crappy job, having privacy was a perk in its own right.

Speaking of privacy, he went ahead and plugged in the number to his special hidey hole, another engineering feat accomplished by his sister's engineer, Sampson. One that allowed Al to stuff away a bottle of the best quality whiskey found on Earth, expensive shit that he'd spent a pretty penny of his savings getting hold of. An uncork, a smell...lord, it was like fire married cherries. A long pour into the glass next to his nightstand, and he measured it carefully. No waste and not too much. He shoved the sealed bottle back into hiding then moved over to his desk with his glass.

First things first, business.

He typed away on the keyboard, summoning up the coding for a private transmission to his black market contact.

Back to Jupiter, planning a stop at Callisto space station for the usual drop.

The words on the screen blinked twice and disappeared.

Moments later in its place came a return message from Rayna, a woman more mysterious than deep space. He'd met her once in person and found the meeting lackluster, though she was extremely prompt in communications.

Thank you for the update. Usual box. Upon receipt of the delivery your payment will be in the usual spot. Deposit in place before arrival.

Al sighed and deleted the message, clearing his data cache and wiping any trace of his contact with Rayna from the limited memory of the communication hardware. Leaning back, he grabbed his glass and took a sip of the whiskey. The chill of the leather against his back, combined with the burn down his throat, sent a shiver down his body. Involuntarily he thought of Loyda, her eyes, the way she'd licked her lips. The towel seemed far too small for him and he could stand to put some clothing on.

A knock on his door came, but before he could stand or react, the door opened.

"Damn it, Mangle—" Any and all speech was lost as Loyda walked in.

She looked clean, far cleaner than she had in the processing room. A floral scent came with her, intoxicating him and sending him backward. He sat naked except for a scrap of terrycloth, and his dick took the bait in front of him. She walked in as if summoned from his every fantasy, a saucy smile to her lips and a twinkle in her eye.

It wasn't healthy, his body's fascination with this woman, nor was it helpful that she'd taken to barging into his room like his first mate. "By all means, come on in."

"Don't mind if I do." She stopped on the other side of his desk and Al slowly sat up straight to provide a little bit of cover. Yet if she dared to come any closer, she might get more than an eye full. "This how you like to spend most of your time?"

"It is after I've just cleaned up from finishing in body collection. Trying to enjoy a little hard-earned privacy, but I guess even five more minutes is too much to ask?"

She smiled wide, and the vision momentarily stunned him. Loyda smiling at him like she'd found all the riches in the known universe was something he had never been prepared for.

"Murderers don't get peace and quiet where I come from."

Al frowned. Such a smile failed to fit her words and with them came a sour taste in his mouth. Her badge fell out of her hand and clunked on the desk.

"While I thank you for saving my life, I am here to tell you that Allied Authority hereby warrants arrest for the crime of murder and that your ship and crew now report to me."

Damn if it didn't feel good to say those words. To let them roll off her tongue instead of keeping her lawful nature in place. She was ready for Al's horrified expression.

Except that frown turned upside down and he started to laugh, loud and boisterous as if she'd told the funniest joke he'd ever heard. No threats, no rising up from his chair to attempt to intimidate her. Disappointment crept into her veins. Al grabbed a glass and tossed back the little alcohol remaining within it. She could have busted him for that too, but alcohol possession attracted far more leniency than murder.

"Knew you were too damn good to be true. A walking, talking temptation sent to ruin me."

"Yes, and your ship is now mine." She puffed out her chest, determined to wrestle back control. To own this moment and be proud of it.

"Can we talk about this after dinner?"

"You're not taking this seriously. I'm talking about jail time, freedom revoked, ship seized."

"And what gets me out of this horrible possibility, Officer?" The full weight of his gaze settled on her, the words spoken in some sultry growly voice which hit her right in the soft spot between her legs.

She did a shit job of covering up her attraction to him. *Fatch.* But hell if she'd let him know how he affected her going forward. No, he'd fall in line or else. "Nothing short of a full confession of all your illegal activities. Even then, you're probably still facing a heap of trouble. You can't screw, shoot or blackmail your way out of this one."

"You don't know me very well then," he replied with a wink.

She ignored it. "And I don't plan to. Get your eyes off my tits and realize I am not going away."

He sat up straight, leaning onto his desk, interlocking his hands. "Then what do you want? Because you could have waited until we were back on Jupiter to spring this shit, with a full squad of pups."

"You're right, and I want you to point this ship toward the Saturn ring jails to —"

"I don't go to jail without due process. I know my parliament rules. You can't just lock me up. Innocent until found guilty by tribunal."

Loyda sighed and debated what to tell him, though Al appeared smarter than her initial assessment. He'd just made the mistake of believing her story. "Not locking you up. There's trouble at the jail — everyone has disappeared…prisoners, workers, and I have been assigned to find out what happened."

"Sure, and now that you've fed me a bunch of lies only to come clean, you want me to believe the most secure site meant to lock up those who have done horrible deeds has been broken into and everyone removed? Lady, you tell some pretty wild tales."

Loyda's hands went to her waist and she stared Al down. "For a man who lies with more ease than it takes to breathe, you calling me a liar is rich. You're right — I would have waited until we were back on Jupiter, if this emergency hadn't arisen."

"Then let's head for Jupiter and your army of pups waiting to take me into custody." Al waved a hand in the air — more signs that he wasn't taking her seriously.

"I saw you and your crew kill four innocents."

Al's carefree face fell. "That was self-defense."

"A parliament jury won't see it that way. Plus, I found a transmission to your buddy Rayna in your system and I am aware you are harvesting parts for black market sale."

Al was fair-skinned, but he looked a step away from space-frozen at those words. He readjusted himself, sitting up straight in his seat. "Guess we're going to Saturn."

She stood and came a little closer. Something about having this man at her mercy, a big beast of a being, hit all her buttons. Again, that pesky *want* fluttered and hummed its way through her veins, as bad as any drug or shine in the system. Circling around the edge of the desk was as close as she dared get, but it still gave her a chance to gloat over this near-naked man.

"Glad you could see reason." Loyda didn't wait to catch his expression, but turned to leave.

A heavy hand clamped around her wrist. "Not reason. *Want*, honey."

She couldn't resist his tug on her, the strength and force sending a thrill of pleasure and alarm through her. Her free hand went to her belt, grabbing for the knife strapped to her calf. As she was whirled around, coming flat against him with her shirt-covered breasts pressed against his hard chest, she dared to glance upward.

Those eyes were blue, deep, deep blue, almost like that of an ocean. "Believe me, as soon as this situation offers me no benefit, I'll be changing the arrangement."

Sense knocked back into her amid the deep breaths they were both taking. Her heart pounded — or maybe it was his heart. Regardless, that steady drum in her chest reminded her of those poor innocents, and she angled the point of her knife against his dick. Lord, that part of him was hard too.

"You won't be the first who hasn't tried some dumb shit with me."

Al chuckled, the sound vibrating through her body like a sexual awakening. It had been a while since she'd indulged in a little careless screwing. But he would be the worst choice.

"I won't force you. I can tell from your eyes I wouldn't have to. No, I like my women to beg me to give it to them. Before this is done, you'll be like every dust honey I ever met…pleading for a fuck."

Al let her go then, and his release allowed her to deliver the final say on the subject.

A solid knee right to his prickly parts. Al groaned and went from standing to sitting in his chair.

"Get Frankie to point the ship on a direct stream to Saturn. And know this—I don't beg."

Chapter Six

Al's towel fell to the floor as Loyda walked away. He silently dared her to look back at him. To see what state she'd left him in. *Idiot.*

She didn't spare him a second look and shut the door behind her. Her government-investigator confession had put him on edge, sure, but the fact that he faced arrest, a tribunal and much worse failed to kill his body's desire to have her, his dumb dick motivated by her scent, her fierce nature and inability to back down. He sensed similar attraction from her, from those deep, labored breaths she'd taken, the way she'd held still with a little tremble against him.

He pressed the button on the ship intercom system. "Frankie, what's our position?"

The speaker let out a little crackle, then a voice he'd had whisper sexual innuendos in his ear many times responded, "About a half day from Callisto."

In times past he would have told Frankie to put it on auto and haul her ass to his quarters to provide relief after a stressful day. No expectations, just sex. Except that urge died on the tip of his tongue. He didn't want Frankie. He wanted Loyda. He wanted to kiss that defiance right off her sweet mouth. To drive into her while she screamed his name.

Fatch.

"Change of plans. We've been asked to take a shipment of emergency powder to Saturn. Set us up and let me know estimated arrival as soon as you can."

"I didn't see a communication— "

"And you weren't supposed to. Get us sorted, now."

"Aye, asshole." Frankie's annoyance was unmistakable in the immediate pulse of feedback she sent back through the system, making his ears ache.

He reached down and grabbed his towel, wrapping it back around him, ready to move into the bedroom and get dressed when his door opened again. "The hell—"

"Just in case you're thinking of backing out, I've got eyes and ears everywhere." Loyda eyed him now, leaning halfway through the door with her hands braced on the door frame. Her eyes stopped on where his hands held the towel closed.

"Already figured. Now, unless you want to start the begging now, I suggest you leave. Otherwise, I won't feel guilty about what happens next."

A light pink blush stole into her cheeks. "Until later."

She left again and he sighed his frustration. Part of him wanted to do the begging, get her to come back and let him look on her as he rubbed out his physical issue.

Al moved into the bed and willed his erection into submission. Thinking about body processing and the cold of space cleared up any lingering desire pumping in his veins.

The door to his office opened again, followed by the door to his room. "I told you I won't feel guilty about what happens if you keep pushing things."

"Really?" Frankie's anger-laced voice filled the room "I don't remember that conversation. What's going to happen? And please let it involve me getting naked."

He turned and did his best to school his impression and ardor. "We don't have time for naked."

"Really? Or is it you are more interested in some young, fresh piece of space meat that brings with her the air of the uppers? Sorry, I don't buy her little 'I'm from Ganymede' story and you're just a typical sucker if you do." Of course, her eyes were on his near-naked bottom half.

Al stepped into the pants and pulled them up, rapidly searching for something to grab. "I don't buy it and told her as much. She damn near got sick on the processing room floor. I told her she keeps pushing for more assignments and to learn things before she's ready, and I won't feel guilty when she quits and runs for the nearest access hatch."

Frankie pursed her lips and she laughed. "You seriously cut her a new one?"

Relief flooded his system. This whole Loyda problem would get him caught in a mutiny if he wasn't careful. "Yes, I did."

Liar, liar. The words and voice in his head were his sister's. He'd told a million lies—ones to protect, one to smooth his path and always those to reduce death. And he'd tell a million more if it meant protecting himself...and Loyda.

Frankie's raised eyebrow made him wonder if he was convincing enough, but she didn't push the subject. "We are en route to Saturn. Mind telling me what the hell is happening?"

"BCS sent an encoded message. They need our latest process of powder at the ring jail."

"But Callisto, your contact?"

He regretted each day involving his crew in the mess of his black market schemes, but after losing Styx, he'd had no choice. He needed to get out of the business fast, and he no longer had the courtesy of sticking to honest work. Honesty had never earned anyone any favors...or so his mother still said to this day. "It will raise suspicions if I disobey a direct order from BCS. I want us rich, not caught."

"Do you think—"

"Less thinking and more doing." Hell, Frankie had been about to reveal the biggest thing he needed kept secret. He'd lost a hell of a lot more than just his ship the day his sister had betrayed him. Tuatha had come bearing promises of a freedom he had never dreamed possible, and a clear slate for him and Frankie.

She came in close and leaned into him. "All right. I got something you can do."

What the fatch is wrong with me? But Frankie next to him elicited no desire, no arousal. He found himself wishing Loyda had stayed. Except appearances had to be kept. He wrapped an arm around Frankie's shoulders and pulled her in close. Pressing his lips to her forehead, he tried to keep things tender, tried to summon forth as much fake emotion as he could for her.

"Let's hold off. I'm exhausted, Frankie. That other crew, the processing...it's been a solar day. I just want food and a chance to take it easy before the next job rolls in."

She sighed, a subtle sign of her trying to keep her thoughts to herself. "Fine. Let's feed the beast then. Maybe you'll change your mind after."

He doubted it. Because his mind was focused on one thing—how the hell he'd turn the tables on Loyda Miles.

* * * *

Loyda secured her door then checked the viewer. Al was back in his room, lying down. Alone. Dinner had been awkward, watching Frankie finger-feed Al, her hands all over him and sitting practically in his lap. Loyda had done her best to pretend she hadn't seen anything. Mangle, Bertha and Duffy had all acted as if Frankie's behavior were normal, which shouldn't have bothered Loyda—but it did. Al had seemed less than engaged but had allowed his pilot's behavior to continue.

Regardless, she couldn't stop herself from grabbing the tube microphone and activating it. She matched the frequency to the receiver she'd placed in Al's nightstand next to the bed.

"Why didn't you tell her the truth?"

Al jumped, sitting up straight, pulling a big-ass knife from underneath his pillow. He glanced around. "Shit, Loyda. It's not nice to start a phantom conversation with a question."

Loyda chuckled. "You're avoiding the question. Why not tell Frankie the truth if you're so close?"

Al scrubbed his face with his free hand and put the knife back in place. "Because I'll have a mutiny on my hands, or she'd kill you and stick you into the processing machine in a heartbeat."

The words short-circuited something in Loyda's brain, warring with her instincts that told her Al was lying, and his actions over the past twenty-four solar hours, where he'd held her close and almost kissed her. The tension between them had lasted even when she'd threatened him with arrest, as he sat in a chair with a towel the only thing between him and bare-ass nakedness.

"I'm not in any real danger — save the 'I am trying to protect you' racket for someone who would believe those lies."

Al shook his head. "You certainly think you're invincible, but with everything that's happened out here in the last solar day, I would expect some of that invincibility to be shaken from your core. Accidents happen — look what happened to those collectors who got on board that ship. Holes ripped right in their suits…improper maintenance."

The threat lingered. She hadn't given too much thought to the idea of danger, blazing through as if her status within law enforcement and as an agent of parliament offered her some sort of protection. On Callisto and other planets, no one dared to touch her.

"Why not tell Frankie and let her get rid of me, then?" That was the crux of it — was he full of empty threats or did he want to be rid of her? She watched the screen closely, seeing that he slept without a shirt, his abs clearly defined. The damn pixilation of the video screen showed the cut muscle. Her mouth grew dry as he lay back on the bed, one arm behind his head.

"I told you earlier, bunny. Want, pure and simple." No tells, no games. He stared straight up at the ceiling as if he could see the very spot where she'd placed the camera.

Loyda swallowed hard, her body fully awake now. *Time to change the subject.* "Do you trust your crew?"

"I don't rely on them. Big difference."

She scoffed. "You rely on them every day. Every job."

Big Al rolled his eyes. "You don't get it. Most of them never do. That's what I want my crew to think, what I want everyone to think. Why are we talking about this? Let's talk about that knife of yours and what you felt when you pressed it up against me."

"I felt ready to stab you in a personal place." Her voice had gone soft and low. She needed to get in control again.

"Really? Adrenaline pumping through you, a powerful feeling like nothing could stop you? The contemplation of what was hiding behind my towel?"

She shook her head, even though he couldn't see. She did it to combat the sly smile he wore. "No."

"I'll tell you what I thought of after you pulled that knife. I dreamed about you telling me to strip. Asking me to touch myself so you could watch."

Goddess, it was getting hot in this room. The engine being so close made the most sense as a reason, though his words lit up ideas she'd rarely entertained. Her relationships in the past had been less outspoken about sexual desires. *More demure.* Sure, on Callisto she often took what she wanted, but it still required more silence and less talk.

"You're awfully quiet, Loyda. Let me tell you that the same thought came to my head when Frankie walked in on me getting dressed. I'd hoped it was you. Hoped you'd come back to see how far things could go.

Hell, I'm getting hard just thinking about it." Al reached down and stroked the outline of his dick in his pants.

Loyda struggled to keep her breath even. She could picture what Al said, vividly. Her demanding his compliance, having him strip in front of her, but...*he's a criminal.* And that was where she had to draw the line—she could never have him. Could never be with him, not in a physical sense.

"Loyda, your eyes and lips are some of the most glorious I've ever seen. Your hair looks soft, and your scent's near intoxicating."

"And you haven't even seen me in anything but work clothes."

Al groaned, pulling his dick out of his pants. "And your voice. Bunny, I'll stop if you tell me too. But it's been a long day and I'm eager to work off a little tension."

She cleared her throat, but the words stuck, with her watching him take his dick in hand. The sight was gorgeous as he stroked his generous, fully hard length, curving upward towards his belly. The damn thing had to be almost an inch and a half wide. It looked like the vitamins they gave collectors made things other than bones bigger...

"I can imagine you watching, threatening me with the tip of your knife, licking those lips." Al stifled and bit his lip.

Her hand hovered over the connection button to the viewer. She could end this right now, let him have privacy to finish his deed. *Fatch it.*

"Keep going." The words were hers, but damn if they sounded unlike her.

He did as she asked, slowing to spread a drop of precum over the tip. "You could give up this whole good-girl routine and come down here. Let me see you. Let me fuck you."

Two hard and heavy pumps into his hand had him lifting off the bed a bit.

"I can't," she replied on a breathy sigh. If she'd only been a regular recruit, a woman looking for a bit of fun... *But I'm not.*

"Oh, you're missing out, but I've got time still to change your mind." His pace picked up, as if he found something new to imagine. As if the end was near. "But not tonight. I'm too wound up to hold out. You'd never make it even if. You. Ran."

A final moan of pleasure and his seed shot out, right past the fatching camera feed. He kept pumping, thrashing against the bed as he did, the efforts showing how sensitive he was. How many times had she been stopped short of pursuing the same result on other men? They'd pushed her away, and here he embraced it, over and over until he collapsed, his eyes closed.

Her smalls were soaked through with arousal, and as his motionless body stayed still, her desire was replaced with concern. "Al?"

"Next time you should really be here."

Chapter Seven

Al jolted awake to the loud squawks and squeaks which signaled an incoming vessel. His quick springing motion to a standing position brought his foot into collision with the corner of his nightstand.

"Fatching hell."

He hopped around single-footed, grabbing for his shirt from yesterday. It would work, since he'd barely worn that and the pullover for two solar hours. He'd been exhausted, but not exhausted enough to stop himself from performing a little peep show for Loyda. *Idiot.*

Stomping through into his office, Al had barely slid his feet into his grav boots before Loyda busted through the doors. She was in dirt-brown pocketed pants, grav boots and a tight little thermal number covered by a vest. If the vest had a few buttons popped open, he'd be able to ogle her breasts and annoy her…the way she was annoying him now.

"APU is doing a mandatory check. Port side in fifteen minutes."

"I know," Al replied, securing his footwear.

"How do you know? The alarm…"

"Is designed with different types of signals so we can be radio silent when need be. You sure you're an investigator, a seasoned one?" He looked at her then, enjoying the laser-eyed stare she leveled at him.

"I can handle this."

Of course, her perusal trailed lower, past the shirt to his pants, and damn it if his dick wasn't hard already.

Al cleared his throat. "I'm happy to let you handle it, but now may not be the right time."

"I meant the patrol." Loyda patted her hip. "I can flash my badge and get this underway."

"Yes, but kind of hard when my whole crew will slit your throat after they find out about your other job. I can take care of things just fine. I travel prepared for any type of issue. You don't think I'd operate without papers, do you?"

She took two steps closer, bringing that elusive scent of hers with her. Some sort of flower. He'd thought jasmine or lilacs, but no. Flowers weren't frequent on Mars, where women, even his mother, smelled more like marijuana and corn shine.

"You're a habitual liar. I'm not sure what you travel with besides disreputable people." Her words should have offended him, but he was right back to reading the heat in her eyes. He glanced at her lips and damn if she didn't dart her tongue out, teasing him with the very descriptive words he'd used last night to describe what he wanted to do to her. Normally these damn rooms were freezing, but suddenly it felt too hot for clothes.

Fatch it. Al leaned forward and whispered, "Let me kiss you."

As if driven by some unseen force, she leaned in as well. Their lips were mere inches from touching when the door to his office burst open again.

"Al, they're minutes from the airlock. Where the fatch are —"

Mangle's words had Loyda moving backward instead of forward, and no way in hell would Al give up his shot now. He grabbed Loyda right as Mangle's last words trailed off. She came flush against Al and he crashed his lips into her.

He'd intended to be gentle, but lack of time didn't allow for it. When she moaned, he came undone, shoving his tongue roughly through the little opening she'd provided with her lips.

The kiss beat out every fevered imagining he'd had while he'd stroked his dick last night. But he had pups almost on his ship, an audience and no self-control.

Al slowed the kiss, pulled back and looked at Mangle to avoid getting caught up in the flush of arousal and desire he knew lingered on Loyda's features. "Next time knock."

"Does Frankie know you're banging the new recruit?" Mangle's arms were crossed and he wore the look of a man scolding a small child. Except Al owned whatever he did, even the stupid things.

Loyda spoke as he did, "We are not —"

"If it becomes Frankie's business, I'll tell her."

Then came the kick to the balls he didn't expect, as Loyda leveled him square between the legs. He groaned and doubled over. Sure, the whole thing probably warranted a slap or two, but not a kick to the prize.

"You're an asshole, Captain." She mirrored Mangle's stance, and it seemed he was destined to piss everyone off today.

"I obviously misspoke. I'll make sure everyone on my ship knows my business."

Mangle laughed. "Al, Frankie is going to act straight bitch to everyone once that happens. Maybe I should take over running things—"

Al rose to his full height. This was the crap he had to prevent. "You can shut your mutinous mouth right now."

Loyda stepped between them. "There's nothing for Frankie to know. It was an argument, nothing more. Captain just likes to rile me up. A little heat and sparks fly."

"Oh." Mangle took a step back, raising his hands up as if to say he was over it. "Well, next time you want to have an argument that ends with *my* tongue shoved down your throat, just let me know." He winked and motioned for Al to come on. "Boss man, it's show time."

He marched forward, passing Loyda without a second glance, but one thing he knew for sure—if Mangle tried to touch her, Al would kill him.

* * * *

"Thank you, sir." Al offered the parting words as the airlock door closed behind the pups.

After they disappeared back onto their ship, Al spat on the floor. "Fatching pups."

They'd done just enough damage, but not enough to expose all his secrets. Tearing up odd areas of the ship, including his galley, looking for contraband. Either they were stupid or they'd been paid off by Tuatha. Still, working with even those most connected guaranteed him no favors. Appearances had to be maintained. No one was above the law or able to skirt through things...unless they were willing to pay. Al was done paying.

He marched through to the cockpit, where Frankie sat staring at the ceiling and twisting a strand of her hair. "Frankie, how long until we hit the stream again toward Saturn?"

"Probably about the same amount of time it took you to dip your dick in Miss New on Deck."

He groaned. This day was turning to shit. His stomach growled in response. He needed food, since breakfast had never happened. Loyda had disappeared, Mangle seemed more tense since the pups had invaded the processing area and Frankie had obviously received word of Al's poor morning choice.

Except he couldn't bring himself to wholly regret kissing Loyda. Her lips underneath his equaled the bright shiny spot on his black-hole day. "Nothing happened, and if it did, I don't have to justify anything to you. Now, alert me when we're almost to the ring jails."

Al left before Frankie could flip him off. His mother would tell him that messing around with his crew would only bring this kind of trouble, but damn if he could stop things now. He entered the galley and found Bertha shouting out obscenities. Al considered leaving, settling for a liquid alcohol lunch, but Bertha spotted him before he could make a quick getaway.

"Hold it right there, Captain. I need to know what the hell the pups thought we were hiding. They've screwed with half our stores — we're going to be eating mystery meals soon. Now, I have to give Mangle space for the organs. Is outer space shrinking?"

Al made his way through the galley, wading past unmarked cans, pots and plates. "Space is not shrinking. That's a conspiracy rumor scam artists use. Quit reading those flyers every time we go to Callisto station. As for the freezer space, give it to him but tell Mangle he's gotta help clean up."

A pot of stew bubbled on the converted space hunk that functioned as their stovetop burner and oven — nothing like the infrared machines on those fancy upper ships. Then again, burnt meat tips never tasted good without the char from a real fire, even if it was chemically controlled.

"But why? We're already limited."

"Because we are headed toward Saturn with a delay to Callisto. Don't need anything spoiling, do we?" Al ladled two big scoops of stew into his bowl before stepping away.

Bertha opened his mouth to speak, then closed it like a fish. Al had seen fish before in a tank, their lives dependent on what their masters fed them. They were all fish. *Until you don't get fed or you decide to adapt.*

He moved out of the galley prep area and into the dining station, to two big tables shoved up against one another with an assortment of stools. Here was where the rest of Al's crew had wandered to. Including Loyda, who eyed him cautiously when he took a seat opposite her. She jumped a bit, and damn if he didn't feel like an ass for earlier. He almost opened his mouth to apologize when Mangle hollered from the other end. "Bertha going to give me that freezer space? Don't want my special meat going bad since those pups screwed up everything."

Funny how he and his crew had learned to talk about body parts as if they were anything but. "Yes, if you help him straighten up the galley."

Mangle let out a groan. "But I'm in the middle of stealing Duffy's take on the next job."

"You're betting money you haven't earned yet?" Loyda's look of disbelief wiped away any apology Al had. The woman, for all her bluster and nerve, possessed too much naivety in areas she needed to appear tough in.

"I don't have nothing else to wager, unless you're offering something up. See, Duffy and I are inclined towards the women only." Mangle's words got Al clenching his fork as he shoved a bit of stew into his mouth to keep quiet.

"Oh, no, my momma always taught me to never risk what you don't have or bet what you're sure to regret giving away tomorrow." Loyda stared pointedly at him, probably in reference to their kiss earlier.

But hell if she hadn't confused the fatch out of him. Did she regret it? Was she alluding to something else? Because he'd been risking everything since the day he'd left Mars in search of a life outside of mining and racing…gangs and death by illness, disease, or injury.

All he had gained so far was everyone having him by the balls. Mainly Loyda and Tuatha, but he'd only let Loyda handle his in reality. The meal dragged on, with slow bites and him wondering what she was thinking, but he couldn't ask her with Mangle and Duffy still in the room. The pair of them were focused on the outcome of their game instead of bothering Loyda any further.

When they finally finished and left, Al was fully prepared to start asking questions. He had a ton of them, but it seemed luck wasn't on his side today.

The intercom crackled, Frankie's audible throat-clearing not helpful either. "I need relief on deck. This pilot is ready for food and a few hours of sleep. I've been flying ten solar hours straight."

Al shoved out of his seat. "That's my signal."

Loyda nodded in response, and that was it.

Fatch my life.

Chapter Eight

Loyda finished her food after Al left, the lone figure in the eating area. She'd spent the day trying to glean as much information from the crew as possible. The pup inspection had been a lesson in ridiculousness and she planned on writing a detailed report of how the pups running random checks were in need of a massive overhaul. Raising her suspicions even more was how they'd failed to do a detailed check in any area where she knew contraband was hiding.

Not to mention the cursory look at Al's papers. And without a warning. No death barge had free rein to travel anywhere near the uppers like Saturn and Neptune. They had routes, and Loyda had seen Al's. Saturn wasn't on his schedule. Upper folks found the barges tacky and distasteful. Why flaunt death? No, all bodies were put out to space, to a collection point a fair distance away, off-planet.

It appeared there were more questions than answers at this point.

"What are you doing in here? Stealing food on top of stealing men?"

Hell, her musings had screwed her over. "Just cleaning up from my dinner."

Frankie stood next to her, a scowl on her face. "On Mars, when a woman steals someone's man, they're liable to get stabbed or shot."

"Good thing I'm not a supporter of stealing." Loyda had avoided this woman all day and now she was starting to wonder if she was in danger from the crazy lady, whether she admitted her real purpose for being here or not.

"Kissing is pretty much stealing."

Loyda backed away from the dish sink, tossing her clean bowl and spoon into the dry rack. *Time to get the hell out.* "Then could you tell Al to quit trying to steal from me? I'd like to keep my kisses to myself."

"Just stay out of my way," Frankie replied before grabbing a bowl and a spoon. "He'll just use you up and spit you out. You're fresh, new and something to play with."

"This your opinion on all men?"

Frankie's stance relaxed and she moved over to the pot of stew on the burner. "A man has yet to prove otherwise, but some are fun to keep around. I've known Al a long time and there's a few things I've learned. He can't tell the truth, he dreams too big and he's quick to use it and lose it. But you do whatever — just don't say I didn't warn you."

"Appreciate the warning." Loyda spun on her heel and near sprinted out of the galley. The mention of the kiss brought everything flooding back. The moment their lips had touched, desire and attraction had consumed her. He'd touched her like he was both eager to devour and fearful he'd scare her away. *Tender, rough, all-consuming.* If Mangle hadn't been standing at the doorway, she had no clue where they would have ended up.

And that's bad.

Internally she had to scold herself, to stay strong. Al threw off her bullshit meter, and there was something to be said that other people in his life thought and believed the same things. *He's a liar. A cheat. A temporary good time with too much risk attached.*

Even as his mouth had rambled this morning, as it had turned towards seduction and wanting to join with hers, those twinkling blue eyes and full beard…the truth remained that they were impossible. She found herself marching towards the cockpit, ready for round two, except this time she wouldn't fall for his tricks. This time she'd be in charge.

The object of her self-interrogation leaned back, his feet propped up on the pilot station dash.

"How far out from Saturn are we?"

Al gave a start and sat up immediately, lowering his feet to the floor. "Far enough everyone can get a little shut-eye, except me. Get plenty to eat?"

"Yeah, then I got chased away by your pilot. Seems Frankie likes warning people away from you." Loyda paired her words with a smile. *Better to have a conversation than provoke a fight.* She needed him compliant anyway.

"Yeah, we've known each other since we were kids and she's always looked out for me."

Loyda leaned against the wall behind her. "I think she's watching out for *me*."

"Oh? Well, makes sense. I'm not the best person in the galaxy." He sat back in the chair again, in a more relaxed state.

"I've gathered that, but I'm not here to get a personal evaluation of your character. I am here to find out how the hell those pups let you off so easy."

Al chuckled. "Bothering you, huh? A barge outside its regular lanes. You seem like the type to be easily confused when you don't have answers. For your record, my barge has been assigned pickups and drop-offs to Saturn before. Special projects for reliable, dependable crew, if we're called upon."

"Never heard of it." She took a few steps closer, circling around so she could see his face, watch his hands…see if he was brandishing some of those tells he possessed.

Sure enough, Al cracked his knuckles. "Then you haven't heard of a lot of things. I keep trying to tell you how everything is different out here. The rules those Uppers follow don't apply, and everyone has a price."

"What's yours?"

He leaned up, face inches away. "Now, that's a loaded question. Instead, why don't you tell me if you're feeling the same thing I am? The spark, the itch. That thing we shared last night."

Loyda shook her head. Sure, an invisible tether seemed to already be attached to Al, and lord knew that if he reached for her, she might go willingly. "That's not something we need to talk about or discuss, because it was a one-time lapse in judgment."

"I love being a lapse in judgment," he replied with a wide grin. Then, thankfully, he leaned back in the chair, putting a little distance between them again. "If we're not going to talk about the attraction we have going on, then tell me why you got put on this shit detail of going to the Saturn ring jail?"

How much of the truth did she tell him? She could stick to the Saturn piece, but she didn't want to mention Tuatha. *Not yet.* "Kind of like your special projects. Boss needed someone to investigate, and it so happens I have a ship at my disposal for the moment."

Al frowned. "For the moment, unless you might want to give up that good-gal routine? Being bad has its advantages."

"Switching sides isn't in my nature." She leaned against the side of the pilot's control panel, her back to the bleakness of space. "You're a means to a pathway, but not the end of this investigation, for sure."

The way he trained his gaze on her, eyeing her from her head to the tip of her grav boots, she started to feel a little hot. Too hot for being no more than four feet from cold, dead space.

"Means to an end… Most women I've met think I can be a very pleasurable way to an end."

"You don't know anything. There's a bigger picture here. I've been tracking a drug and the creator of that drug on Callisto for months. Did you hear about that?"

Al shrugged. "Wasn't that something Grecia was involved in, the dead cartel head? My sister stole my ship because she got mixed up with Morales and his bid to deliver drugs for Grecia."

"It's more than just a cartel leader and a stolen ship, Captain. It's the hordes of missing people and bodies on Callisto and Io and Ganymede."

He shrugged. The bastard shrugged as if those dead people were no big deal. "People go missing every day."

"And you don't give a damn about them?"

"Nope."

She crossed her arms and damn near growled. "What if one of them was your sister?"

"She got what she deserved." The small crack of his pinky knuckle gave him away.

It was unbelievable this guy would not give up his bad-boy front, the persona he donned to fight through every day, no matter the cost, even with his sister's life possibly in the balance. "Well, that's not what all of them deserved, Captain."

She shoved off to a standing position and came to a halt in front of him. *Screw proximity.* He needed to feel a little more something, anything. "Some of those people missing were husbands, wives, mothers, brothers, people with loving families. Not deadbeat druggie nobodies that you're used to interacting with. The numbers of missing continue to grow and the only tie I have to all of it is one name…Tuatha."

He adjusted himself in the seat, no longer leaning back, and she wondered if that was because she was wearing him down. If, maybe… "Do you know Tuatha?"

He cracked all his knuckles right in front of her. The man was oblivious to his tells. "Never heard of her."

"How do you know it's a her?"

"I don't. It's an instinct to refer to an unknown person as the gender of the person you're talking to. Read that in one of those fancy medical docs they send out for supplemental training through the BCS, all about understanding your crew and being relatable and shit. Didn't help me relate to my sister or her problems, or her urge to steal my damn ship. Maybe if she hadn't, I wouldn't be in the situation I am in now."

Of course he blamed his current predicament on his sister. Another reason her body needed to slow its slip drive. She didn't need to be all revved up for a man who couldn't take responsibility for his own life and issues.

"She ultimately set me back."

Loyda almost felt sorry for him, a man hung up on the things of his past. How many had she met like that? *Too many.* "From?"

"Early retirement."

Loyda laughed, expecting to hear the familiar crack, but nothing. She glanced at his hands, silent in his lap, then decided to take a step back. She was done with fruitless conversations. A mattress, even her threadbare one, would be more comfortable than continuing this pointless lesson in circle talking. "Liars and thieves never retire. They just find new ways to steal. Good night, Captain."

She pivoted around him and the chair, heading for the exit. In her quick departure she almost missed his whispered comment, "One day you'll call me by my real name."

Chapter Nine

"Satttturn is where I wanna be. Rings are what I wanna see. Ice baths and sulfur sands call myyyyyyy name."

Al opened his eyes in alarm, arms flailing against the bed. *How the hell did I get here?*

He remembered the heated debate with Loyda and the fact that he'd lied through his teeth. How he'd turned to working on his sweater again after she'd left. A million knits and purls later, and Frankie had relieved him as his eyes started drooping.

Frankie halted her serenade and croaked through the speaker. "Al, respond. You need to get up here. I don't know if we can dock or if we should, because there's no one answering hails."

He pressed his intercom button on the nightstand, regretting the fact Loyda was probably hearing everything. Al really didn't want to deal with the woman yet, or face the continued sexual frustration and reality that he couldn't be the hero she seemed obsessed with. "Give me five. Just keep trying to hail. If it doesn't work, we do a manual landing."

Climbing out of bed, Al took a minute to stretch. He'd been hunched over in that chair for hours then balled up in his bed under the sheets. The farther they got away from the sun, the colder everything became. *Maybe that's why Uppers are so heartless.*

He reached for his pants first, and had barely pulled them up past his knees before Loyda opened the door. He could tell it was her by the scent of flowers that came with her. Once his pants were secured, he turned to face her. She was looking all around the room, a pale pink flush across her cheeks from the clear look she'd gotten at his bare ass. Going by her apparent blush, she must have liked what she'd seen. He grabbed a clean shirt out of his closet, taking his time.

"You have a problem with barging in on me when I'm damn near naked. If you didn't want to get an eyeful, you could just watch your little spy video and wait a minute."

"We need to talk before you head up there."

Yeah, they needed to, because he could see Loyda trying to bust in and take charge. That was something he couldn't afford. "I agree."

Loyda's head reared back. "You do?"

"Don't look surprised or nothing, but yes. I need to make sure you understand that I'm in charge. And we need a cover."

She nodded. "I'm good with that. Keeping my role under wraps is important. You could say we're headed over to investigate. If it's an illness or something, better to expose the fresh space bait than anyone else."

Al cleared his throat. "Is that something we are worried about? Illness killing people?"

Hell, no way would they step foot off the ship, her investigation be damned. He wouldn't die for strangers, wouldn't endanger future populations by carrying back some diseases like an egg incubator.

"No, of course not. If this was a possibility of an infectious disease, they would have sent someone completely different to handle this mess. Besides, in my experiences with the large amounts of missing people, it appears drug overdose is the most common cause…so I still advise that we don't touch—"

"Ah, ah, ah, now just stop there. Let's not say anything like that. We leave it as we're going over to check things out. At least get the main recording copy of all jail records for the office, then we come back. At that point, if we need backup, we'll call for Duffy and Mangle. No options. If we find ourselves exposed to anything threatening, we have the ship detach and send out a distress beacon."

She held up her hands. "Okay, I'm aligned, but I would like to do more than just grab a recorder."

"We'll be on camera, my crew watching for signs of trouble. Unless you see something that requires immediate need, you stick to the plan. And even then, loop me in. Don't go off guns blazing."

"How do you know I would do something like that?"

He smiled. *The nuggets on her.* "Call it captain intuition. I've been around enough crazies to know people who can't be trusted, people who go off half-cocked and those who enjoy being day savers even at the risk of everyone around them. You, pink cheeks, are a day saver."

He couldn't help himself reaching out and trailing the blush on her face that re-emerged with a vengeance as his finger traced the ridge of her cheekbone. *Fine damn structure. Too damn good for Mars trash.*

So, he drove the knife in. "So much for being the good guy and hating liars when you're actively lying to my crew."

Loyda pulled away from him. "Go fatch yourself. And stow the flirting crap. I have enough to worry about without wondering when you're going to try and sneak in some sort of kiss or touch."

She had him there. He needed to back off. "I'm sorry. I need to practice more self-control. I'll admit I tend to lose it a bit when I'm around you."

"You barely know me."

If that wasn't a slap in the face. Okay, most of his reaction to her was purely physical. The first time he'd ever felt that way about a woman...where she occupied his waking and sleeping thoughts. Yet he thought she experienced something similar. Maybe he'd misread things. "You're right. Let's focus on the task."

"All records, audio, video, data logs. We need to know when these people were here last. They have been missing for at least two solar days."

"That kind of data extraction takes time. And I don't have the proper equipment."

She grinned. "But I do."

"Great. More reason to give the excuse that you're coming with me." To say the situation left him off kilter was an understatement. He'd lied again, to her. The smuggler's hold was filled with bone power for Tuatha's men. Powder he was supposed to drop off here at the jail after he swung by Callisto. "You can extract the stuff quickly, like under a solar hour?"

"Yes, the equipment we have is state of the art, the best government scientists can develop. I can do it in half that time."

Al glanced up and down her. "Where do you hide that stuff?"

"Wherever I need to." And she called *him* horrible for flirting.

This whole situation was out of his depth—investigations, missing people... He was a collector, a knitter and a once-upon-a-time ship tinkerer. And now someone in deep shit if he didn't casually find out what had happened to Tuatha's people, as well as find a way to get that damn woman the powder she demanded in return for his continued freedom.

"Let's get a move on, then."

They hit the bridge first. Frankie looked skeptical. "No way I am docking against that thing. Manual or no. It's too risky with no one controlling the connection on the other side."

The churning in Al's stomach got worse. "So we take a shuttle. You keep Acheron at a close distance, but far enough away so there's no danger."

"Do we need to be worried about something?" Frankie raised an eyebrow as she stared him down.

"No, but you know how I like to be cautious."

"What if stuff goes wrong?"

He knew what he'd said to Loyda, but there was more at stake and he didn't feel ready to give up on living just yet. "You send out a distress call. You get help, but you don't leave us. Got it?"

"That won't fly with Mangle."

Loyda didn't look confident and neither did Frankie.

"You stay even if he puts a gun to your head."

Frankie shook her head. "Should have made me first mate instead, or taken me to bed instead of the recruit here. At least I'd feel the sacrifice was worth it."

"We're not—"

"Don't make me regret this, Frankie." Al grabbed Loyda by the arm and pushed her toward the door.

Frankie called out after them. "Don't screw us down there. And you might want to find out what the hell happened fast."

* * * *

The red docking light switched to green and Loyda breathed a small sigh of relief. She was a ball of nervous energy, like a solar flare popped off the sun, hurtling through space.

Loyda had always worked in a world where trusting people came with risk. Except, she had enjoyed the company of at least one or two people she could rely on. In this scenario, she had no one. Sure, Big Al was all flirtatious and eager to get in her pants, even claiming it as his motivation to keep her alive, but...

"You're awfully quiet for someone about to go into a jail missing all its prisoners. Figured you at least be telling me what your expectations are, or excited to get me so close to bars." Al chuckled as he hit the button that released the belts locking him into his seat.

"Just focused."

Or worried you're going to try to kill me. Loyda was prepared, with weapons in multiple places and hand-to-hand combat training, though she liked to avoid using the skills unless necessary. She'd become all too comfortable with inflicting pain and meting out violence—which was what she wanted to prevent.

"Or trying to come up with ten different ways to disable me or prevent me from leaving you."

Her mouth dropped open and she clamped it shut.

"Yeah, I told you I'm familiar with people. Where I'm from, you have to read people and learn to predict motive. So, let's clear the air." Al stood and shifted in front of her. The proximity brought warmth to her body where she'd lacked it before. Space was too damn cold.

"I've got plans for us. Lots of them, involving us both naked. A kick to the balls, a slap to my face, insults…those don't change anything, except my determination to win you over."

She risked looking up at him, the heat reflected in his gaze washing over her. Physical attraction didn't equate trust, but in this instance, she sensed and believed he wanted her enough to fight to keep her alive until he got to have her.

Which he never will.

"You believe me, then?"

She swallowed against the lump in her throat and licked her lips. "Yes."

"Good." He pressed the release button on her safety belt and took a step back. "Let's get this crap finished, then?"

"I'll follow you."

Al eyed her with a raised eyebrow and cleared his throat. "What about door codes? I don't know those."

Fatch, habits die hard. She'd been ready to put herself at a distance still. "I'll take lead. Good call."

She maneuvered past him, some of their body parts pressing against one another. Okay, her breasts brushed his chest and she reacted in an inappropriate manner. Except she had to stay serious, focused and act like her stomach and entire being weren't in a riot. "So, how many women have you been with? Frankie's comment got me curious."

She heard the crack of Al's knuckles before he answered. "More than you can imagine."

A personal question didn't always warrant an honest response. But how a tiny part of her wished he would trust her in such a way.

"Loyda, I get it. This whole situation is weird, awkward and relying on people is hard. But know that I want to get us both back to my ship whole and alive. Believe in that one thing and take a deep breath."

She grabbed on to the kernel of truth there — the urge to live — and focused on that rather than the heat of his body behind her as they made their way to the exit hatch.

"At this point everyone has an agenda."

"And I've told you mine."

She typed in the code to the keypad that communicated with the jail's docking system. It beeped in success. "You've told me what you plan to do with me and my body. But otherwise I don't know your end game."

His voice was close behind her, the warmth of his breath against her hair. "My plan is stay alive and free...however I can make that happen. That may involve me telling you some things if we get out of here."

The docking port butted up against the hatch let out a hiss as the tunnel pressurized and made the air breathable. The shuttle rocked gently in answer and Loyda steadied herself by grabbing hold of the shuttle wall.

"Things?"

"Don't ruin it. Just know I would rather head back to Callisto with APUPs backing me up instead of operating against me. And that's my agenda in all its glory. We good to go?"

"Everything reads normal, but I think we should suit up to be on the safe side. I don't trust any information coming from the jail."

So they suited up, full coverage like they had when they'd gone over to the derelict ship, though that time they'd slid across on a tether and this time they secured their grav boots. If something went wrong with the tunnel, they wouldn't be flung out into open space.

Goddess protect us. Her stomach nearly dropped when she took the first step. But everything stayed steady under her feet. She tromped her way towards the opposite hatch. The keypad buttons beeped in order as she pressed them, her breathing a bit labored. Nerves were ridiculous, and after this adventure, she would need to rethink future space travel and assignments.

"Definitely a planet or moon woman," she muttered.

The hatch hissed and wheeled open. Loyda stumbled inside the jail and Al followed. She heard the door roll back into place then felt a hand on her arm.

"You okay?"

She nodded. There was no way she'd admit to her nerves where Frankie could hear. "Let's get moving."

Chapter Ten

Loyda shrugged Al's hand away and moved toward the blinking lights. She saw no people, no bodies—nothing as she made her way down the hall.

"Should probably draw that stun gun if you're going to take the lead."

She glanced back at him. "Worried?"

"Thought we discussed how I like to be prepared for all possibilities." He'd already drawn his own gun and took his time glancing into open rooms, then a side hallway with a sweep of the weapon.

She drew her weapon more for his peace of mind, though the lack of sound and people did start to bother her as they moved farther into the jail itself. Lights were working, though certain portions of hallway appeared darker. Yet every guard station, every hallway was devoid of life. The gauge and meter on her arm kept signaling that the air was safe to breathe, but until she reached the main control room she refused to give in to the potential for false readings.

She passed by one hallway and Al let out a low whistle. "Wrong way, main control is two doors down this way."

Loyda backtracked. "I distinctly remember it being this way."

He winked at her. "There's a short cut."

Before she could step forward, Al took the lead, charging down the hallway. *A man on a mission.* The second door opened easily, and Al stepped through, disappearing. She slowed her stride as she came closer, hesitating until he called out, "All clear."

This room normally held six officers at any given time but appeared as empty as the rest. The camera monitors were all running and echoed a similar horror story. No people, no bodies…just nothing.

"Where the hell is everybody?"

Al scoffed. "That's what we're here to find out."

Loyda shuffled over to one of the holo-tables and started working away at the screen. She extracted the cord to the recording drive on her belt, removed the drive and set it on the table. A plug here, a password there and she was in. Downloading every log, every video, everything from the last three solar days, which according to the screen could take up to twenty minutes.

Dumb technology.

A paper logbook to the far side of the table caught her eye and she reached for it. It took a little bit of a stretch, but she grabbed it with a grunt.

"You okay over there?"

She glanced up at Al's back. He faced the camera screens, moving through them in rapid succession as if searching for something. "Yeah, just checking out this logbook. It's going to be a few minutes on that download."

"Kay. Frankie, are you seeing all this?"

The pilot's voice came through with a small buzz of static. "Yeah, it's like ghost-ville in there. You sure you're not missing a body or two?"

Loyda didn't bother to answer. In fact, she tuned everything out as she traced with a gloved finger the names of the ships that had docked at the jail. One of the ships belonged to Ambassador Anu, an ambassador she'd known for years on Saturn. The older ambassador had inherited his seat from his father at round the same time as her parents had also begun serving their life-long terms.

What the hell is an ambassador doing here? Or his ship?

"Hey, I think I see movement out there." Al's revelation broke Loyda's distraction and her head snapped up.

"Where?"

Al pointed at the camera screen. "Out there, two levels below in storage and processing. Loyda, seriously, there is someone there."

"The download is almost done—"

"Stay here. I'll be back." Al didn't wait for her continued objection—just took off out of the room, headed for the lift.

Chill bumps broke out over her skin and she shifted around the holo-table to get a look at those cameras herself, to watch Al's movements. "Al, this isn't the time for radio silence."

"And I'm not going to give it to you. I'm entering the lift now. No signs of power issues. Everything looks good and is in working order. You'd think there would be signs of fighting, distress, something."

Loyda gave a half-hearted laugh. "Yeah, and I don't like discussing that crap while I'm standing here exposed and alone."

"The space bait is scared." Frankie's voice cackled in glee.

Oh, how I'd love to smack her around. "It's a matter of self-preservation."

"Hit the lower level. You know, I bet I could make good flash off a fist fight between you two ladies. What do you say, when we're back on Callisto—"

"Stuff it, Al." This from Frankie, thankfully.

A part of Loyda was tempted to agree to the idea just to spite the other woman. *I bet I could take her.* A lone beep pulled her away from the screens and she moved back to the holo-table. The download was complete. She took a minute to make sure she disconnected everything correctly. Her luck needed to be less luck and more intelligent performance. So far, she'd failed miserably at working undercover…and staying aloof to one annoying, incredibly sexy captain who kissed like something beyond this universe.

Wait a minute. "Files are all done. Al, did you make it to the spot?"

Lack of words and the soft crackle and hiss of static greeted her in return. She swallowed hard, ignoring the growing tumble of her stomach. The temptation to call out his name warred with the desire to give him adequate time. Her movements a bit frantic, she scrambled back to the camera screens. He wasn't in any visible frame and she pressed the arrow key on the control panel, desperate to find him.

Finally, she gave in. "Al, say something!"

More seconds ticked by, her heart pounding in her chest like that of a death knock.

Then a laugh. A small thing that turned into ridiculous laughter. At her expense.

Al came into view on the processing center camera screen. "Just screwing with you. Imagine if we were doing the deed like Frankie keeps implying. You're close to begging as it is."

Loyda swore. "You're a piece of space trash, Al. Did you find what you're looking for? Because from this angle, there's nothing. You pulled a damn prank on me, like some stupid kid. We don't have time for this."

More silence, and she saw rather than heard Al move around. He started to walk through the processing room door and halted as if seeing something horrible. Her heart stuttered in her chest. "Al, what is it?"

"Listen to me closely, Loyda. Grab whatever you have and run for the fatching shuttle. If I don't meet you there, take off." The gravity in the tone of his voice got her feet moving before he finished talking.

She was shoving the downloader into her belt as she hustled out of the door, multi-tasking and picking up speed. "What's the problem?"

Al's breathing sounded labored and she had no visual, but she imagined him running. "This place is rigged to blow."

Al's lungs were damn near ready to collapse as he made it to the shuttle doors. He pressed the button and sealed everything shut. No glancing around or worrying where Loyda was. Nope, he had to get away now. Though before he could press the emergency release, he stopped and took a glance around the shuttle. Loyda stood only a few feet away.

"I thought I told you to leave without me." He barely got the words out between shallow breaths. *Fatch, I'm out of shape.*

"I decided to give you an extra sixty seconds."

Too damn long.

An explosion vibrated through the shuttle, knocking them both down. Loyda struggled to a standing position first, attempting to pull the lever that would break the seal between the docking appendage and shuttle. She yanked downward once, then twice.

"Shit. Al, why is nothing happening?"

Fatch it all. "The clamp is pinned to the umbilical tether. That's the only reason that damn thing wouldn't work."

"Then we force our way out." She turned and started to move towards the pilot seat.

"Bad idea. We'll rip a hole in the side of the shuttle. I have to go through the bottom hatch then cut us loose with a torch."

"Torches don't work in space."

Al summoned his best smile, given that he was about to put his life on the line again. "Allow me to prove you wrong."

He got to his feet and moved to the back of the shuttle. There on the floor was an emergency escape hatch. It also worked great for sneak attacks when needed. "I hop in here, you seal the hatch and I go out the other one. I'll tether myself to the ship, maneuver around and cut the damn shuttle loose. You be ready. Once I do, you slam that trolling motor and get as far away as fast as you can."

The shuttle shook and shimmied like an unsteady asteroid as another blast occurred within the jail.

Loyda shook her head. "No. What about you?"

"Who gives two shits? Just take off. I'll be connected with the tether." He reached down and opened the floor hatch, mumbling, "if the damn thing holds together.

"Frankie, I hope you heard my orders. You better not blame her." Silence met him as he climbed down into the hole where another piece of metal separated him from space. "Loyda, we've lost connection to the Acheron. So play it smart."

She glanced down at him. "Just hurry up."

The hatch door slammed shut, the lock clicking into place. His cue to get moving. A couple of twists and a shove and he flew out, barely holding on to the door so he didn't launch into space. *Getting laid isn't worth this much.*

Damn, he needed to get them out of here and, for probably the second time in his life, he was grateful for the abnormal bone structure and body he'd grown thanks to years of the space supplements the BCS required employees to drink. Those things gave him the strength to pull his body around against the weightless part of space. To get his grav boots locked on the hull of the shuttle. The tether latched, and from his new vantage point the Saturn ring jail looked like a miniature sun, flares of light popping off as more of it exploded.

"Loyda, I am secure and moving for the clamp. Are you seeing this?"

"Yes, we are running—"

A big piece of debris effectively cut off communication as it plowed into the shuttle's main window. Al couldn't breathe, the air in his helmet gone thin at the idea of Loyda—

Fatch. He shook his hands and his head, clearing away the fear, the helplessness. He needed to get the clamp loose and that was exactly what he did. Scrambling as fast and as safely as he could across the hull, he pulled the torch from his belt, covered both it and the clamp with a plastic seal and struck the flint. The thing popped like a mini laser igniting flesh. Within seconds, the hold of the clamp on the bridge released, the shuttle floating away from the jail.

Al reversed course, but it would take too long to get to the hatch, to get back inside. Besides, the oxygen in the shuttle had already been compromised, so he made his way across the hull, over the main entry hatch and to the busted window. Loyda lay in the pilot's chair, unmoving. He struggled to bust away some of the window glass to make room for him. The piece of debris wouldn't budge. The struggle from his shaking hands and arms. For a man always in control, he'd lost what little he had, thanks to the woman lying prone before him.

If only he could get to her, help her. The only good thing was that her helmet seemed to be in place. Al finally forced his way inside, the shuttle itself in a small rotating spin—no power, no engines, no sway over the tides of space. He fought for balance and gained it when his grav boots locked to the floor.

Her helmet wasn't secure. Loyda's chest rose and fell in rapid breaths with her desperation to take in what little breathable air she could. Al tried to be gentle as he worked to get the helmet in its final resting place. Once it clicked and the air began to flow, Loyda's eyes shot open, her gasps of breath deepening.

Al reached for the communications button, flipping the switch and sending silent hopes they still had a limited connection. "Frankie, if you can hear me. We're free floating and need pickup."

Another explosion rattled the shuttle, this one bigger than the last. He let go of his hold on Loyda. She appeared to be getting control of her breathing and sat back in the chair, pushing herself to a sitting position.

Al focused on the dashboard, the gauges and switches. They needed a working vessel, or at least a trolling motor. A few switch flips, a dial turn here, a good slam on the dash and the shuttle rattled to life.

"Hang on, Loyda. We're getting out of here."

* * * *

Loyda leaned back against the headboard of Al's bed, cursing her bad luck. She should have been in her quarters. "Why am I here again?"

Al stood near the door, holding two steaming mugs. "Seemed the best place to keep you comfortable?"

He approached slowly and extended one of the mugs to her. "You were oxygen deprived, might have died. I feel a bit guilty and gave up the comfort of my bed."

"I would have been fine in my quarters." She took the mug, trying not to appreciate the familiarity, the domestic tone this little scene held. They weren't to be. They'd both almost died. "Tell me again what happened. It's still a bit hazy."

Al nodded and took a seat in a chair across from the bed. She shouldn't have appreciated it so much, but she did. For all his bluster and his imposing manner, he granted her space and a little respect. Maybe oxygen deprivation wasn't good for her ethical sense.

"Well, the jail was rigged to blow. We hightailed it out of there, but after the explosion, the shuttle docking clamp didn't come loose. I had to go out and cut it out myself. Tricky business, and in the middle of that some debris crashed through the main shuttle window. That's when you got knocked out. I'm not sure why your helmet wasn't secured then — probably not enough time. It's amazing you're still alive. When I got to you, you were already passed out." He paused and took a long swallow of whatever was in his mug.

Loyda did the same, loving the sting of the heat from the hot coffee. It'd been a long time since she'd enjoyed such a fresh cup. "Go on."

"I was able to get your helmet in place. Get the trolling motor working, and we made it back here to the Acheron. Frankie, Mangle, Duffy and Bertha were all happy to see us." He cracked his knuckles against his thigh. "You were awake, but you passed out again…been pretty much sleeping for the past solar day and we are taking a slow creep around one of the Saturn moons. A smaller, uninhabited one."

Dread rose up from deep in her stomach, a sick feeling that danced with the hot coffee there. "But my evidence, my data retrieval from the jail."

"Anything left is long gone. The whole place is up in smoke. Lucky for you, that fancy data device you brought with you is still intact and undamaged, from what I can gather."

The rough and tumble in her stomach subsided. "Has anyone tried to contact the vessel?"

"No, but the crew are getting antsy. I've been lying to them, told 'em I'm waiting on BCS direction, since we were witness to an act of treason or, worse, terrorism." He downed the rest of his beverage, but

Loyda hugged her mug close, enjoying the heat seeping through the porcelain.

She still felt cold, muddled and in desperate need of taking some sort of action, because nothing made sense. "There's been no APUP cruiser? No one to investigate the explosion?"

"No."

Everything about this screamed *wrong* to her internal radar. Any other situation so close to the Allied Parliament would have warranted an entire armada of cruisers assigned to the location. Something to signal awareness.

"I need to call my boss."

Al set the mug down. "I think we need to come up with a better plan than alerting parliament's investigative division to exactly where we are."

"You don't understand." Determination filling her, she set the mug on the small table next to the bed. The same one where she'd hidden her audio device. Then she swung her feet over the side, so they were touching the floor. "They should have already responded. They should be en route. The fact that they're not is even more concerning, and we may have a huge problem headed our way."

Hands came up to grab her arms and for a moment she wondered if Al would push her down, try to stop her. Instead, he lifted her to a standing position. "This isn't my problem. It's yours. And your government's."

"They're your governing body, too."

Al chuckled, moving to brush a stray lock of hair from her face. "No, afraid not. I'm Mars born and raised — we all know that parliament cares even less for us than those on the moon. They use us as they see fit but provide us no representation at the big table. I have very little faith in parliament, but if you need to contact someone, then so be it. All I ask is that you throw in a good word for me. I did save your life."

He released his hold on her and took two steps back.

There were a million things she wanted to say, a million more she wanted to know, and the universe sure had horrible timing. "I need a pad from my quarters, please. Can't risk my message being intercepted or someone from your crew overhearing."

"It's in your quarters?" Al grabbed both mugs.

Loyda nodded.

"I'll be back, then."

By the time he returned, Loyda had taken a seat at Al's desk chair and started working on wiring a patch in through the holo-screen on the desk.

Al secured the door, then turned. "Heads up."

He tossed the pad toward her. She caught it with ease and pulled up the program to get the patch running. Everything worked seamlessly and, in that moment, Al seemed more like a partner and not a person desperate to avoid jail time or worse.

The opposite end picked up faster than she expected, except the face that greeted her wasn't her boss. "Investigator Miles reporting in, sir. Where is Captain TK?"

"Seems you're surprised to see me, when you should know exactly where he is." The grisly, narrowed-eyed expression of the Investigative Commander soured the coffee in her stomach. "He's dead, Miles."

"Dead." The word silent and mouthed from her lips. Unreal, when he'd appreciated her willingness to go to the Saturn ring jail days ago. "But he can't be."

"He is, and you are expected to turn yourself in at the Hermès station immediately." The commander signaled to someone off screen and Loyda double-checked her measures. Everything still implied they couldn't track her.

Al still stood across the room, but his arms were crossed and his eyebrows bunched. If anything, whatever confidence she'd built with him before was failing fast.

"Sir, with all due respect, I am on an assignment with the Saturn ring jail, ordered here by the very man you say I killed and—"

"We know all about it. It's detailed in some pretty damning evidence, plus an anonymous tip. You won't be getting away with any of this. Your idea of justice against those who break the law is a bit vigilante, even for our organization. It won't be tolerated."

Her head spun. The *room* spun. She'd woken in some alternate reality where everything was upside down. Maybe it was a joke, a big one, on her. Except, deep down in the pit of the same stomach that could pick a liar out of a crowd, reality didn't escape her.

"Transmit your coordinates, Miles. We will have a ship pick you up immediately. You will be able to prove your innocence in the tribunal, if you truly are innocent—"

Loyda pressed the button to end the transmission and cut off that annoying man's voice. Her hand shook as she brought it away from the pad.

"Well, that was interesting."

She looked up at Big Al, his face going a bit blurry from the water gathering in her eyes. "Why?"

"Because it looks like you're on the wrong side of the law now…just like me."

Chapter Eleven

Loyda swiped at her eyes to rid herself of those pesky tears. The damn things always came running when she got angry or frustrated. She shoved out of Al's chair and started pacing.

Frustration wasn't the half of it.

"Hey there, it's only a comment about being a criminal. Doesn't mean anything. I'm just giving you a hard time. No way you killed your boss...unless you have some network of killers at your disposal. I might want to hire one of them— "

"Can you shut up, so I can think?"

Al raised both hands in mock surrender as he walked past her. "Sure thing. Don't let me stop you from brooding...because that's what you're doing. Thinking? Well, you can do that out loud for the rest of us."

She sighed. "Really? Like you give a damn."

"You might be surprised." He sat and started messing with her pad, disconnecting it from his holo-screen. "Give me a shot."

"This whole thing started on Callisto. The ink, the deaths, missing people... I was supposed to track those responsible. This was supposed to be my big case." She stopped short of tracing down those childish thoughts. How this would be the one that got her the recognition to prove her abilities to her parents. To show them she could do so much more outside of politics. "The trail led me to you, to some sort of smuggling operation tied back to the disappearances. Ultimately, when my boss mentioned the Saturn jail, I thought—"

"You thought it might be all tied together. Super thin, Loyda." Al pulled a desk drawer open and started digging.

"Yeah, well, the number of bodies makes sense. This person or persons doesn't work in small batches. They like big numbers."

And now she sat on the verge of being labeled a killer, a vigilante seeking revenge. She had to call her parents.

"I need to make another call." She marched back toward the desk chair, to the screen and her pad.

"To whom? You call anyone, you're putting us all at risk. You're wanted now."

"You don't understand. My parents—"

"Will happily turn you in."

Her stomach curdled. *Never.* Her parents believed in her. "No, they'll be devastated." Her gaze wandered to Al's hands, which were now in possession of two large copper-colored needles and a ball of red yarn. "They need to hear from me first. What the hell are you doing?"

Al glanced up at her. "Knitting."

Silence reigned for a moment. Al shoved the stuff in his hands back into a drawer. "Fine, you can make the dang call. But your encryption isn't the greatest. I think we can double down on it. Besides, I'm taking more risk by letting you do this. Your little hang-up-on-them stunt made them even more desperate to catch you."

"How do you know that?" Her hands went to her hips, her mood on the happy rise from angry to defensive.

"It's exactly what happened every time I pissed off a pup or someone in law enforcement over the years. They don't like the word no."

"My parents may know what to do." Loyda refused to continue chasing the path of thoughts that led to the worst possible outcome. She couldn't live in that world, a world where she would be branded a criminal. If anyone knew the laws better than her, it was her parents.

Al's hands worked magic, dialing up code and inputting signal modifiers. Then he reconnected her pad. "All set. Still wouldn't recommend that you keep this on for very long. Ten solar minutes max and the risk of them dialing back a trace increases."

"I haven't been in contact with my parents in a while. They weren't big fans of my choice to become an investigator, so we don't talk too much. I doubt the pups are going to think I'd contact them."

Al rolled the desk chair back a few inches and stood. "Whatever you say, space bunny."

Loyda took the seat and shook out her hands before wiping them down on her pants. Somewhere in the last couple of minutes, she'd gotten nervous. Her parents were already disappointed in her — this would top that initial disappointment in a big way. A deep breath and she pressed the button. The opposite line rang just a few times, then her mother's face came into view, followed by her father's. The one she didn't expect to see was Gaylord's.

"Maman, Pater, I have some bad news."

Her mother clicked her tongue. "Bad news is putting it mildly. The office of investigation has already told us. You are implicated in the murder of thousands, and your boss. This is very grave news and —"

"We're shocked, Loyda." This from her father, who clutched her mother by the shoulders. Both her parents, ambassadors in parliament, had only represented their families with honor, as had their relatives before them. The Miles line had never possessed a whiff of a scandal or wrong deed. This could ruin everything generations had worked for.

"Why is Gaylord here?"

"As your fiancé, he has every right to be present. They came to him as well."

Gaylord shook his head. Her fiancé, whom she'd rarely seen in the last four years.

Loyda sat up a little straighter and kept her face smooth from desperation. "None of it's true. It's all lies."

Gaylord sighed. They never talked, never exchanged anything more than the functionary greetings when required. He was her mother's choice for replacement of her seat, and to keep things in the family, they had agreed to an arranged marriage. Her parents had. Gaylord...wasn't unappealing. He had a strong physique, firm jaw and piercing gray eyes, but his lack of emotion made him suspect in Loyda's mind. "Loyda, if what you say is true, then you have to turn yourself in. You can't continue to be a fugitive from the law. The family lawyers will represent you, help find the falsehood in these tales. Though your lack of communication with me and the family doesn't help your cause."

Loyda glanced up and Al stood there on the other side of the desk, trying to appear innocuous, but the smirk on his face had the opposite effect. She wanted to curse at him.

"Loyda, focus on us. What are you doing?" Gaylord's words brought a frown to her face.

"Nothing." Except still getting treated the same way, as if she isn't an adult capable of making her own decisions. She was in her mid-twenties with plenty of experience. She'd survived almost dying twice in less than three solar days. "Turning myself in will only guarantee I never set foot on Saturn as a free woman again."

All three members of her family, her supposed allies, erupted into chaos. Not a single one of them supported her blossoming idea…one that grabbed hold of her like a clamp to a docking bridge.

Her father scoffed. "See here, young lady, you can't continue to put your mother through this."

Cue mother's outrage. "Through this, the family future is at stake. Think of more than your precious investigator career that doesn't matter."

And Gaylord's begging. "Loyda, see reason. Please…our marriage, your family name…everything is on the line. You have to turn yourself in — you must."

All those intermingling statements were exactly why she chose that moment to disconnect the call.

Big Al's grin was a mile wide, and she hated how he'd been right. That they would expect her to go against everything she believed, that they would think the system she'd seen let so many people down over the last couple of years would somehow do right by her now.

"You can stop grinning like a madman and appreciate the fact that you're right."

"Oh, that's not what I'm grinning about. The parent thing I could have called a mile away, since you come from such straight, upstanding folks. No, I'm smiling because like I said before, Loyda, you're stuck with me. Oh, and welcome to being one of the bad guys."

Big Al believed he had a little bit of good luck running with him. Surviving an exploding jail, a wrecked shuttle and now having Loyda stuck on his vessel at his mercy. The balance of power had altered, and he could negotiate his way to whatever he wanted. Forget telling Loyda anything about his raw deal and side gig with Tuatha, or that he had a good feeling that the sick, twisted bitch was the person responsible for the blown-up jail and stolen bodies.

"I'm not a bad guy. I'm a good woman being framed."

"There's a difference?" he replied with another grin.

Loyda still hadn't given up her spot in his chair. She looked a bit vulnerable sitting there, swallowed up by the overstuffed cushions as she started to work away on her pad again, pulling the damn data storage device from her pocket. "There is, and I intend to prove it. I'll need your help, though."

The woman was daughter to ambassadors, from the conversation he'd overheard. And she had a betrothed. Which put a damper on his wooing plans… *Liar.* Okay, nothing put a damper on those, since she wasn't officially married and didn't even have a ring on her finger. Al had long ago accepted his lack of goodness, and damn him for wanting to corrupt Loyda further, especially because she was determined to fight things so much. He'd show her that being bad wasn't all that horrible.

"Help with what?"

She pointed to the holo-screen. "Going through all this video and the data I got from the jail. I need to figure out who did this—whoever did also killed my boss. They want me out of the way and any seasoned investigator would see this for what it is."

He shrugged. "And?"

"It's a set-up."

Al laughed. This woman was something else. "Most investigators wouldn't say that. They'd see this as a neat and tidy open-and-shut deal. Sometimes the obvious answer, the easy one, is the right one."

The frown on Loyda's face almost made him laugh again. "Except it's not. I didn't kill anyone."

"Though half the time I think you're looking at me with murder in your eyes." He came in close to her and crouched down next to her in his chair, in his space. He liked it a lot. The same way he'd liked bringing her coffee in his bed. *Damn.* "What do I get out of this 'helping' deal?"

"What do you want?" Her breathing slowed, stuttered, the pulse point in her neck pounding. It was maddening, this thing between them. But he had time, time to draw her in. She'd be begging.

"You."

He let that word linger between them, the tone of his voice hopefully telling her all the thoughts racing through his head. To find out what that first kiss had promised, the foreplay they'd experienced on the tether, in proximity, when she'd watched and listened to him come. Except he wanted it gradually, no pouncing or crazy rush to a finish.

"I want us to ditch this whole 'I'm your boss' or you threatening me with incarceration. Let's forget that I'm a body collector who may be up to no good and that you're working with the pups. We're just a guy and a woman in mutual agreement."

Loyda held out her hand. "Okay, fine."

He almost leaped up and shouted, but managed to keep himself under control. He reached for her hand, eager to come into contact with her, but she pulled back at the last second.

"As long as I can see your papers."

Al stood up. "Medical records? I'm clean. I get checked out every—"

"No, the papers you showed the pups to convince them to let us proceed to the jail."

"Is that all?" Al moved away from her, back into his bedroom and to the safe. He dialed in the combination and removed the packet of papers, the ones he'd used a dozen times, that gave him access to wherever the hell Tuatha wanted him to go. "Here you go. Look over them to your heart's content. I'll be back to help you in a few. With your fugitive status confirmed, we need to get this ship moving the hell away from here and Saturn."

She grabbed the papers and started skimming through them. "Where will we go?"

"For now, the safest place a bunch of criminals can go…Callisto."

As he left, he didn't miss her sharp intake of breath or the fact that she didn't offer him any other words.

But revelations could wait until he got this ship headed as far away from where the pups would be coming as possible.

Chapter Twelve

The announcement to the crew came and went with little attention and fewer questions. In fact, Al sensed a feeling of relief from everyone at the mention of returning to Callisto. Except the movements appeared to make Loyda more tense. She'd holed up in Al's office for more than a day, reviewing data and video. Al had stepped in as he'd offered to help, but he could only take so many solar hours of staring at a screen before he had needed a break. She barely spoke to him and the entire time he doubted the sincerity of her handshake. *Should've kissed her, you idiot.*

He hadn't then and didn't now. No, he gave her space to chase her killer and try to clear her name. He could sense her identity was super important. Al had long ago given up any ideas and misconceptions of making a name for himself or becoming something more than the son of a pair of race gang lords on Mars. His fate was determined by what he did to provide for himself, and that came from making crinkle.

"Surprised Mangle hasn't barged his way in here. Or Frankie, for that matter." Loyda's sudden words nearly made him jump off the chair where he sat knitting.

Yes, he'd given up hiding it. Had grabbed his bag halfway through that morning and continued his work on her sweater, each row a chance for him to blow off the rising frustration from Loyda's silence. Now she'd decided to speak. "They were informed you were still space sick from lack of oxygen. Which this wild-goose chase you're on is the equivalent of."

He'd brought her food and drink, watched over her. Made sure she was comfortable and moved her to the bed after she'd passed out in front of the holo-screen. It was unnatural for him to do such sweet things, because that was what they were. But he'd been raised by two people who were naturally cruel to others but had always done their best for each other. Lifted each other up. *No sense in looking into it any further.*

"You would think such a thing." She made the statement as if he was the lowest of low, the bottom of the barrel, and he'd had enough.

He finished the damn row and tossed the needles and yarn aside. "Before I get looped in with the worst of people in your mind, would you care to tell me what the hell happened between our handshake and when I came back into the room? I thought you were in a mood, but obviously I screwed up somehow."

She looked up from the holo-screen, her gaze narrowed. "Who's Tuatha?"

Al cracked his knuckles.

"No, no bullshit. Stop thinking about lying to me."

"Loyda, I wasn't going to lie."

She shoved herself out of the chair and circled around the desk. "Yeah, but the knuckle cracking and the mention of my name says otherwise. You're a horrible liar, Alexander. You have the worst tells. I spotted them on day one."

He stood up as well, offended by the accusation, but more upset that she could tell when he wanted to hide something. "You've got some nuggets for calling me out like that."

"And you've got none for constantly running from the truth. Just be honest, for once in your damn life."

Al sighed and looked at his hands, at the truth there. He would never escape this, and maybe, for once, telling someone what had happened wouldn't be so horrible. "My sister, Toni, really screwed me over stealing my ship, Styx. Didn't help that she got led on by that crappy husband of hers. Selfish bastards, the pair of them. I was already doing black market deals for parts. Had some extra things stashed on Styx that got discovered when the ship was impounded on Callisto station. When I went to get the ship, Tuatha was waiting for me."

"Who is she?" Loyda came closer and took a seat on the small couch he had against the far wall. It had plenty of sitting space, but for some reason he sat down next to her, drawn to her.

She was no longer standoffish but concerned.

"A woman with a lot of power. Pissed off at my sister and Morales for their betrayal of Grecia, for a lost drug shipment, and she needed a body processor...a death barge. I tried to refuse, but she's a scary bitch." Al grabbed for his needles, the yarn...focusing on something as his mind wandered back to that moment. To the moment he'd realized he'd lost more than he'd ever planned. Tuatha was the epitome of selfish and self-serving, and damn anyone who got in the way.

"She rattled off the names of my entire family, every person who'd ever worked under me on the barges, and vowed to kill them all, including me, if I didn't agree to her terms. So I made a deal. Though it was just like Momma always said, you lie with a viper and you'll get bit."

Loyda reached out, her hands on his arm and sliding up and down in a comforting motion. "What do you mean?"

"We processed bodies for Tuatha and dropped the barrels of powder with men stationed at the prison, after we sold body organs on the black market on Callisto. But now everyone is gone."

"Understatement of the universe. It's here on the tapes. Men garbed in black, faces covered, marching wardens, prisoners, jailers, all to the lower processing levels, then they disappear. No toxin, no gas…they just accepted their fate. And I've got an ambassador's ship landing at the prison hours before these events happened." She launched off the couch and started pacing. "Tuatha… she's got to have connection to the ambassador."

"Wouldn't surprise me."

Loyda kicked at one of the chairs. "You could have just killed her, Al."

"That's illegal. Do you hear yourself?"

She pounded her fist against the desk. "But then she'd be stopped. Still doesn't make sense why she's killing so many people."

"It doesn't have to make sense. Often killing doesn't. Only thing is that she seems strong in her convictions, and a person who believes in what they're doing is more dangerous than someone who doesn't. Now, quit beating up on my furniture."

The gap between them closed again. He sensed her heat and smelled her scent versus seeing her, his focus still on the last few pieces of the chain.

"What the hell are you doing with those needles?"

"Making a sweater. I mean, it's pretty self-explanatory."

Loyda took a seat next to him again. He liked that, her sitting close to him. "Yeah, and pretty ridiculous. Old women knit, not virile ship captains. We are so screwed. Who knits anymore?"

"Captains of death barges who like to give crafty gifts do."

"Who's the sweater for?"

Al didn't miss the softness to her voice, and he stopped knitting, stroking his beard with one hand. "A woman I met on Jupiter. Loyda, she's a beauty. Redhead and fiery like me. She's got legs as endless as a slipstream. A set of… Eh, she's a true beauty."

All lies, when all he could picture was Loyda, writhing, wearing nothing but the damn sweater he was halfway finished with. A big, off-shoulder thing by the time he was done, and it would caress her skin with as much appreciation as he had for it. To guard her from the chill of space.

"I know you're lying, but for the moment it's damn attractive, you trying to hide this from me. Tell me another story." She laid her head against his arm, too small to come up to his shoulder.

"How about you tell me one instead? Like something about this fiancé of yours."

Loyda chuckled, and warmth filled him at the vibration her laughter carried through his body. "It will bore you."

"Try me." He struggled to pick up the needles again, not wanting to disturb her place against him. The domestic feeling of this moment wasn't lost on him. They lived in their own little universe in this room.

"Fine, but don't say I didn't warn you. I'm the daughter of two ambassadors, which means that when they both retire, only one of their ambassador positions passes to me. It's the rule—you can only pass on one seat to your offspring. Most families have two children, but my parents only had me. So I've been raised to take my mother's place. My father's seat must be passed to someone else."

"You got a cousin, don't you?"

Another laugh. "Parliament politics like to keep things between married couples—less possibility of dissident thoughts if your spouse is also part of the process. Also, you have those second children who can't get seats the traditional way. That's what Gaylord is. A second son, unable to inherit his mother's seat because his brother's already getting his father's seat. My family came to agreement with Gaylord's many years ago and arranged our marriage."

"Should be criminal, telling someone who they can marry or be with."

Loyda sat up and he stopped knitting to look at her. "Why? It's beneficial, prevents people who have no interest in running or learning about our government from getting spots in parliament, keeps young girls and men in those upper positions from making stupid decisions to marry someone who can't provide for them or act as a true partner."

"I can see some of that, but sometimes the heart wants what it wants."

"Sentiments of those looking for a silver lining where there's nothing but heartache and sorrow."

And she calls me cold.

Al refused to argue, but he'd grown up on a place of heartache and sorrow. From what he vaguely remembered, love got a lot of folks through the pain, helped them refuse to be burdened by it. "So, they arranged this marriage — then what? Why aren't you living the life on Saturn in marital bliss?"

"I wanted a chance to change the world in person, not by passing laws and governing from afar. I struck out on my own path with the agreement that this life as an investigator would only be for a couple years. The truth is, I'm not fit for parliament, as much as my parents expect me to take up the mantle. My tour of duty as investigator has gone on two years past the deadline and I've been searching for an alternative option ever since."

He reached for her, waiting as she looked at his outstretched arm and hand, as if trying to determine if the embrace would be worth it. Then she came to him, folded up against him, and the contact, her scent, the warmth of her body was perfect. "I know something about expectations, parents wanting you to follow in their footsteps even against your own dreams. I've found only one way to chase off the guilt when those particular emotions come knocking on my mind."

"How's that?" Her words were muffled against his chest and he loved it. Loved the feel of her hot breath seeping through his shirt straight to his skin.

"Fucking."

She glanced up at him then — perfect timing, because he was done waiting. Done trying to remember what that moment had been like before when they'd kissed.

This time when their lips met, when the space between them disappeared, it was like the damn explosion at the jail…hot and on its way to scorch them both. She was addictive…the softness of her lips, the way she moaned against his mouth. He wanted to be able to pull away first, to break the connection, but couldn't.

The only thing that seemed to break through the mating of their tongues was a heavy male voice clearing its throat in some fake guttural cough. Al knew exactly who stood there interrupting the one moment he'd been waiting over a week for. *I'm going to put a lock on that damn door.*

Loyda was the one to break the kiss, not him. But he spoke first. "Go the fatch away."

"We have a problem."

Mangle stood awkwardly by the door. Not with his normal comfortable manner, with the smirk and the light to his eyes. No, this was Mangle afraid, the only reason Al moved away from Loyda and stood up from the couch.

"Hopefully this won't take long."

She didn't say a thing, just sat on the couch, her legs tucked up underneath her. And Al wondered what the hell he'd gotten himself into, when leaving this woman for a few minutes made his chest ache.

"Your timing is the stuff of nightmares, Mangle. I had her right where I wanted her." The hottest kiss of his damn life—not that he could say that. No, Al had to play it cool. *Keep calm and all that poster shit from old Earth.* He walked beside Mangle, heading for the cockpit. "What the hell was so important you had to pull me away from that?"

"It's not fucking good, is what it is." Mangle didn't say another word as they marched into the cockpit, where every crew member had gathered.

"What's with the committee?"

Frankie whirled around in her seat. "This bullshit right here." She pressed down on a communications button and the bulletin pulled up on the main holoscreen.

A female voice repeated what the words said. "The death barge Acheron and its crew are wanted for questioning by the Allied Planetary Union Police. They may be harboring a fugitive. Consider this vessel and its occupants armed and dangerous if you encounter the vessel on radar, at check points or docking anywhere in allied space. Please report this information to your nearest APUP outpost. A reward will be issued to the informant with information that brings the fugitive, Loyda Miles, into custody."

The words were more than he feared. Sure, he'd expected the pups to come after Loyda, but not him, his crew or his ship. They were all in a shit load of danger. "There may be some reasons for this."

Duffy stomped his foot. "I'll say, Captain. It's our future on the line. I mean, what the hell?"

Those words set the whole room erupting, multiple voices crying out in outrage and confusion, but the last one, from Mangle, was mutiny. "Then let's turn her in. Be done with this mess. We can get the reward."

"Hold up just a fatching solar second. Loyda is on the run from government agents. She confided this to me, and it's now compounded by what she and I saw at that jail."

Frankie reached for him, but he took a step back. "What happened there? You haven't said a fatching peep besides to go circle some uncolonized moon and now to head to Callisto."

No, he'd kept it all to himself, because if they were being hunted, keeping his crew in the dark gave them a chance to deny involvement. Except that didn't really matter now. "Everyone is gone. Dead. Marched into those incinerators with no looking back. We haven't figured out the why, but Loyda is trying to, and the who as well. Someone did this and they can't get away with it."

Bertha pulled off his beanie and scratched his head. "Cap'n, it looks like they already did get away with it."

"Yeah, but we can try to fix this."

Mangle slapped his leg and laughed. "She's got you by the nuggets, wound up so tight you'd spill crinkle on the floor to get a taste."

Anger boiled beneath his skin. His flesh felt damn hot. "Shut your mouth."

"No." Mangle stepped forward, his smaller stature nothing compared to the height and bulk Al had. Some people who took the supplements got big, and others, like his first mate…they didn't get anything. It still didn't stop them from being assholes. "I'm not backing down. The woman in your quarters is a pup. And she's going to get us all killed."

Al cracked all his knuckles on both hands. "No, she had a brother there and they're trying to frame her."

"I've had just about the last lie I can take. We were supposed to turn things over to Tuatha. This was the last damn trip, then freedom." Mangle drew down before Al could react, and more weapons were drawn. Frankie on Mangle, Duffy on Frankie and poor Bertha, who hated choosing sides, stood there, wringing his hat in his hands.

Bertha visibly swallowed. "Gotta stop, guys. Pups will win without having to lift a finger."

"What will it be, Al? We all get shot or you turn this thing over to me?"

Chapter Thirteen

Al had experienced a lot of moments during his twenty-plus years alive that could be pulled into the bullshit category, but this one topped it. He'd been in plenty of standoffs with people not willing to part with the dead, with gamblers not wanting to face the fact that they'd lost, with ship captains who'd refused to pay for repairs during his youth on Mars, but never had he stood with a gun pointed at his head by someone he'd considered a friend. He didn't trust friends, but that wasn't the point.

Most people would be scared having a gun pointed at them. Not Al. Instead, he got pissed. Pissed at the idea that the people he protected with his life would dare threaten him. Al clenched his fist real tight and launched it before Mangle could react, right into the fatching spacehole's nose. Mangle howled. "Shit, my nose. Damn."

Then Al grabbed the gun, snatched it right out of the idiot's hand, and one by one aimed and pretend-fired at every person on the bridge. "Here's how it's going to go. We are helping Loyda. In return, this crew will be in the clear, as well as the ship. Mutiny, I can't deal with right now. I know none of us enjoy relying on anyone, but I want to make it through this to the end, alive." He pointed the gun at Mangle, who now held his nose with both hands. Al couldn't tell if Mangle was bleeding, but he really didn't give a shit if he was. "For you, my spacehole of a first mate, try some bullshit again and your ability to breathe will cease."

"Fatch you."

Al cocked the gun, the hammer going all the way back. The silence on the bridge could have rivaled the quiet of space. "Say something else."

Frankie stepped in between them. "He's done, Captain. Do I stick with heading towards Callisto?"

Al still got a good view of Mangle over Frankie's head. It wouldn't take much to move her out of the way. "Plot a course on runner routes, make sure we avoid all pup patrols and checkpoints."

"That's like a three-day trip," Bertha moaned.

"Well, then get comfortable, and I hope you trust these idiots more than I do." Al didn't miss Frankie's hurt look, but as far as he was concerned, they were all culpable, since no one had jumped up to disarm Mangle or dissuade him from launching his idiotic attempt at a takeover. *But no sticking around for excuses.* He left the bridge faster than he'd arrived.

"Impressive." Loyda's voice had him spinning on his heels, ready for an attack, gun aimed out of reflex.

"Shit, Loyda. I could have shot you."

She reached for the gun, resting her hand atop the barrel and guiding it away from her. "I don't think you would have. I'm surprised you didn't shoot Mangle, though."

He shrugged and turned away from her, heading back towards his quarters. The last thing they needed was the crew to start questioning Loyda. "We may need help, an all-hands-on deck situation. Mangle doesn't like me, but he likes living just as much as the rest of us. You figure anything new out?"

Thankfully, she followed behind him. "Maybe, but I need an APUP network computer to determine if I'm right."

Al scoffed. *This gets better and better.* "How the hell are we going to get access to one of those?"

"We're going to break into the Callisto outpost office."

Loyda followed Al all the way back to his quarters, still in a bit of awe at his strength and calm in facing Mangle with a gun pointed at him. Al had appeared undeterred, unyielding, facing that kind of challenge, and she'd wouldn't voice her thoughts out loud, but it had turned her on like nothing else, to the point that she'd just admitted to being willing to break the law, to hack into government computer systems. She was plunging off the deep end, as her mother would put it. Loyda laughed.

"What's so funny?" The both crossed the threshold into his room, and he shut the door, locking it as she walked farther in.

"My mother. I'm planning on breaking the law and all I can hear is her voice in my head rambling on how about how I've lost it, I'm dropping off the deep end."

"You know how I deal with parental expectations?"

Her stomach flip-flopped and she pivoted to look at him. The lust in his eyes was indescribable. "You fuck them away."

"Yes," he replied with a slow nod. The gap between them closed — she was unsure if he moved or if she did. Did it matter? *Hell no.* "It's the best recommendation."

"Then do it. Fuck those expectations right out of my pretty little head." They had three days, if Bertha's moaning was any indication. *Maybe three days is enough to rid myself of all this want.* She made the first move, reaching for him and mashing her lips against his, followed by biting at them, seeking entrance.

He'd made her want this — at least, that was what she tried to convince herself of as he traced random paths up and down her back, her bosom, gripping her ass. All she focused on were the sensations and how they made her come alive. She wished she could launch right out of her skin, rid herself of this desire to get closer, be closer.

"Are you sure you want this?" He mumbled the words against her lips, between the kisses.

"Yes, keep going." That got him lifting her up. Hoisting her in his arms, cupping her ass without breaking the connection between them. There was something to be said for a man tall enough to bring her up to his level, and to move her around like she weighed nothing. It hadn't been important to her before, but after this... "*Oof.*" The breath rushed out of her as Al tossed her onto his bed.

He stripped off his shirt. "One more time — you sure?"

"If I was any surer..." The words died on her lips as his shirt came off. If she thought he'd held appeal to her before, something about the baring of his body, the scars crisscrossing his chest, spoke to the forbidden. How the only men she'd seen naked were pure, clean. This man had tattoos inked into his skin, bits and pieces covered with different designs.

"Now, let's get you out of those clothes." He came over to the side of the bed and motioned her to him. She went willingly, reaching for him, to press her hands against his warm chest. Like a damn roaring fire — that was how hot it was.

"Take my clothes off, but hurry."

He shushed her as he took away her shirt, tossing it aside. "No rushing. To erase the bad propaganda — crap your parents have ingrained in your brain over the years — takes time."

Those words echoed in her mind as he slowly divested her of all her clothing. She should've gotten colder as each layer came off, but instead she heated up. Every part of her became hot, tingly…and sensitive as hell, if her hard nipples were any indication. Other men had never made her this way, driven her nuts, trailing fingers up and down her arms, legs and finally her breasts.

She moaned. "Please."

"Since you asked so nicely."

Loyda couldn't help herself. She watched as he put his mouth to her nipple, taking that sensitive part of her inside him, and near jumped off the bed at the sensation.

When he pulled away, she stopped herself from moaning. She wanted more and didn't want to beg, but was damn close. Then Al put on his own striptease, removing the rest of his clothing. His dick… Well, she'd be lucky if she could walk straight after what came next. And she didn't mind the possibilities. Concentrating on the physical kept her grounded, because she kept wandering to feelings, emotions, the things she'd never really experienced until right now, and she didn't want those comparisons. To know that after they parted ways, this might not happen again.

Finally, Al was bare, and he joined her on the bed, at first beside her, then hovering over her. Their skin touched in places, the weight of his dick heavy and thick against her thigh. This would be something else, and her breaths came in deep inhales and slower exhales.

"Has your fiancé ever kissed you?" Al trailed a hand along her thigh, up between her legs.

She opened her mouth to respond, struggling for an answer, but lost the words when he slid a finger between her labia.

"Here. Has he kissed you here?"

Loyda swallowed hard. "I don't think he cares about kissing me anywhere."

"I would if I was him. I want to and I'm not him. Do you want me to?"

She couldn't find the words, her mouth gone dry and her stomach non-existent like dark matter. All she could manage was a single nod, and he slid his way down. His strong, rough hands spread her wide and this man of unknown depth and strength dipped face-first straight to the core of her. He'd barely begun before a shudder racked through her, before her leg muscles tightened and she felt like someone on a G-force spinning machine about to lose their mind.

"Fuck me, please!"

Chapter Fourteen

Al was fatched. *So fatched.* He'd lost it from the moment they'd gotten back to his quarters. The realization that he could have some peace and quiet, and get Loyda to himself since they couldn't do anything until they got to Callisto, sent his libido soaring. He had her naked in his bed, worshiping between her legs and bringing her to orgasm so fast... Hell, she begged him.

He kept licking, kept working his way through the alphabet, tracing the letters over her clit with expert precision. But each time she started to rev up again, like a slip drive ready to boost into slipstream territory, he would slow down.

Her lightly tan skin, smooth and supple every-where... This skin spoke of something forbidden. Skin that had never known the touch of a harsh Mars wind. Skin not marred by the scars that came from living in dangerous places and traveling through space.

To see his callused laborer's hands gripped around her thighs unleashed something primal in him. Like the early inhabitants of earth — cavemen — they were called, and he wanted to act like one. Possessing someone in that most naked of ways.

Right as she was on the cusp of another orgasm, he stopped. Now was the time, his chance. He rose over her and slid his way into pure bliss. There was no better way to describe what he was getting ready to do. Couplings had always been something *quick fast hurry* with no time to relish or enjoy each other — not that he cared to. She was the first he'd ever wanted to take his time with. The first he wanted to leave a mark both physical and emotional on. He wanted her to feel half of the torment she inflicted upon him without ever knowing. So instead of plowing into her, he entered slowly, letting her feel the strength of him, the length of him inch by hard inch. She moaned and thrashed her hands, hitting the bed.

When he was finally fully seated, she exhaled then moaned. And nodded. He couldn't take that as the only permission. He knew how big he was, knew how women had struggled during intercourse with him before. And while he wanted to mark her, he didn't want to hurt her.

"Can I move?"

"Yes, quit torturing me." Her response came with a smile. He wasn't quite sure if she wanted more of the torture or less, but the patience that he had wielded throughout this encounter was slowly draining away from him. She was tight silky heat wrapped around his rock-hard dick. It was something he hadn't had for a while, and even Frankie complained when he tried to fully enter her. Loyda was different, in every shape and form and fashion of the word.

"Move, Al, please." Now she was begging, and that pleased him to no end. He'd said she would. It prompted him to start to move. A slow slide out and a shudder rippled through his frame, sending a tingling up his spine.

He plunged back in and she let out a little whimper.

"Are you okay?"

"Yes, just fuck me. Pound those expectations right out of my body."

And he did, hoping to replace every stupid expectation her family had given her with pleasure and multiple orgasms. It didn't take long for her to crest again, and as she tightened around him in response, his dick signaled that the end was near. He wanted to stay inside her but knew that that would be risky—his mother had always told him not to ever share his seed with another woman unless she consented to it.

At the very last possible second, he pulled out and splattered her abdomen and breasts with his cum. He couldn't help but admire her lying there, covered in his sex. She drew an index finger through some of it on her breast and brought it to her mouth.

"Fuck, that is so sexy, and I wish we could do it all again."

"We have three days. We can do it as many times as we want."

He grinned at her. "Then let's get started right away."

* * * *

Two days — that was the amount of time Loyda had spent in Al's quarters. She hadn't left since they'd arrived after Al's tiff with the crew. For those solar hours, they screwed and ate whatever food Al grabbed from the galley. Of course, they had to come up for air sometime. Her talented lover appeared to have the stamina of three men, as much as he'd helped her discover the multiple positions and places 'fucking away expectations' could be completed.

After countless orgasms, and with their arrival on Callisto imminent, the primary activity turned to talking.

"So, you're telling me someone in parliament removed everyone from that jail. Or killed everyone in that jail."

Loyda brought her knees up to her chest and hugged them. "Not just the jail. There are missing persons across six moons. Hundreds, possibly thousands of people, and that jail had over six hundred."

She shivered a bit from the cold in the room, a cold she couldn't escape anywhere traveling through space. Al slid an arm around her shoulders and pulled her against his body. "One person being responsible for this whole thing seems a bit..."

"Unrealistic. I know." The whole 'talking this out with him' seemed crazy. But somehow Loyda drew comfort from speaking the ideas tumbling around in her brain.

"That wasn't what I was going to say. More like a hard food cube to swallow. The people don't like to hear when an Upper is doing the wrong thing. And the rest of us know that bad shit is happening but there's nothing we can do about it."

Al hugged her close and she soaked up the warmth. This was something she didn't have with another person—connection. Someone to bounce ideas off, to share thoughts with. Sure, she had her fellow investigators, or she used to. Yet this type of conversation was far more meaningful then the surface-level stuff everyone else always focused on.

"Regardless of what people are willing to accept, tell me what you think. Everything points back to this Tuatha, and a parliament member's cruiser was at the jail. How those two people tie in together, I'm not one hundred percent sure. I need someone just to tell me I'm not crazy."

"Oh, you're as loony as a shine-slinging boozer."

Loyda punched him in the stomach area, but without any force behind her effort. "Truthfully."

"The truth is you have a solid idea. It's close—"

"But. There's always a but."

He chuckled, the sound vibrating through her body, and she wanted to cocoon in that noise. Laughter, true laughter, amid peaceful moments like this had been few and far between since she'd left home. Even during her childhood, her parents had often been serious and not of the mind for just talk without purpose, or cuddling.

"But you're working too hard. Seems we have to work on proper distraction methods, and you know how we do that?"

"You pin me to the bed and drive that big cock of yours into me until I scream."

"I like your thinking, but no. I tell you stories of how I've been screwed over since birth and you eat something. I brought plenty of cubes down, plus some sort of soup or stew—some liquid-based savory thing

Bertha concocted. You've barely touched anything the last two days and I want you strong enough to handle my big—"

"Whoa, you're getting a bit cocky." Loyda laughed.

Al joined in. "You said it first. Now, food."

Al scrambled off the bed and set about loading down a tray and bringing it to her. The soup, the cubes, a big bottle of water. Like they were playing house, on borrowed time. She should have objected, but with every moment they shared, she found herself less than eager to end it, to let it go. For all the trouble she'd gotten into, Loyda had finally decided she deserved whatever she could grab hold of with both hands, and in this case, that was Al.

"Nope, stop thinking." Al put the tray in front of her and pointed at the food. "Eat, drink and listen."

"Aye, aye, Captain." She picked up the fork and stuck it into a cube. Space protein was truly something else.

"Now where to begin… Guess we can start with the fact I was raised by one of the biggest gangs of racers and miners on Mars."

Al leaned back against the pillows and she enjoyed how he tried not to stare, tried not to watch her eat.

"Being the son of gang lords meant I had just as much to live up to as a member of parliament. I was supposed to be the heir apparent, the one to take over after my parents were done. Except I didn't like that idea. Didn't want to spend my life leading some miners' gang."

"Really?" Loyda tried not to laugh. From everything she'd seen, Al loved being in charge and telling people what to do.

"It's true. I know it doesn't look like it from your current perspective, but I never—or I wasn't always—a captain."

"What brought you to this life?"

"I'm getting to that. I think what brought me out here was a combination of things. It started with my parents forbidding me to work on ships. See, Mars is mining, it's racing and it's building those big old ships for the government fleet and the BCS. A builder's life is lucrative...or at least it can be. Except my family had never produced a builder. They produced leaders and my father and mother would be damned if I wasn't going to be the leader they needed. Except the way they led was questionable, and I couldn't stand some of the things that they did. Yet it's funny how leaders don't take it nicely when you criticize how they lied. So instead of sticking around to watch them pimp out my sister, I left. Hopped on board a ship headed for Jupiter and didn't look back. I thought I could get on with one of the finishing companies, but none of them would take me without training and apprenticeship or references. And once you leave home, it's not all family connections. It's find a job or starve. In the BCS, I had a job."

What he described sounded bleak and depressing, and Loyda was very happy that she'd never experienced such a thing. She had seen plenty who had, plenty unwilling to sign up for government work and those who would take to the streets stealing, conning or selling their flesh.

"You were smart. Not a lot of people would've taken the route you did. Most of them are too proud to take such a risk."

"You may be right, but I can see why they don't want to risk it, because indentured servitude isn't a way to win or live your life. I found out pretty quick that I wasn't going to make it being an engineer or a pilot or a body processor, even though I did all of those things throughout my years on barges, and I did my damnedest and worked my hardest to get to the top where I would have some semblance of control and freedom."

"You make it sound like an awful way to live, but the BCS doesn't have slaves — they have employees."

Loyda's comment came from a place of ignorance, but it irked him like no other. "They made the propaganda pretty good if you believe that."

Loyda pulled away and sat up, positioning her body to face him. "I don't believe anything beyond the idea that we're free. We make choices and sometimes those choices are the wrong ones."

"Choosing to fill a belly over starving is the wrong choice?" This from the same woman he could sink into oblivion with...the words he could not reconcile with the woman he thought she was. They really didn't know each other.

"The path you take to get the full belly could be a wrong one. Selling drugs, killing people...I would say those are wrong."

Al scoffed. "Wrong because the government says so."

"My parents taught me ethics. Right versus wrong — it's inherent."

Al shook his head. "Ethics have no place in a universe like this, where right versus wrong changes per person, per situation. Ethics is subjective."

Loyda frowned, and he wished he could wipe it away, but she needed to wake up.

"We could run in circles with this argument all day. While I love a good debate, I don't want to fight you. The current incarnation of this government saved the majority of humanity. We all survived because they made sure the planet couldn't get taken over by aliens, forced us to evolve."

"They trained you well." Al almost got up out of the bed, his urge to get away from her almost equaling his desire for her. "It's more pro-government bullshit. The Earth was dying. They figured out terraforming but needed the resources of Earth to jumpstart things. The rich bastards running everything would never share. I sure the hell wouldn't want to. So they only brought their friends to this new, big world or the people willing to pay everything to be a part of it. It's a giant conspiracy that brought the new government to power."

She raised an eyebrow. "We will have to agree to disagree, then."

She stood, letting the sheet fall, her naked form erasing all argument from his idiot brain. He should have seen that for what it was, a distraction. But hell, he needed a distraction. The coming days would bring either a solution to all his problems or the end to him breathing.

"There's one thing we can agree on."

"What's that?" She ran her fingers through her long hair, swiping it over one shoulder.

Damn woman was fully aware of what she did. Of how she affected him.

"We make some wonderful things happen in this bed."

She came back to the mattress, crawling on all fours toward him, the sexiest woman he had ever seen. "Then let's stop talking."

Chapter Fifteen

"Paging the captain. Docking approved on Callisto station. We will be fully moored in less than ten solar minutes."

Al sat at the galley table, scarfing down some sort of vegetable food cube scramble that Bertha had put together. Another night spent with Loyda and he'd decided to give them a little space. Check in with everyone, get the mood of the ship. His mood, until the awkward conversation the night before, had been buoyant. Now, it was a mixed bag of gold flash and scrap. He wasn't sure if she was someone he could trust, with her ethics flag waving high.

Duffy walked into the galley and dropped a big duffel onto the table. Al's bowl rattled.

"How's engineering?"

"The ship runs like it always does. But I've been too busy to worry about that."

Al shoved his empty bowl aside. "What the hell are you talking about?"

"We're getting ready for a fight, Captain." Mangle marched into the room, his tone as arrogant as his manner. "You've got us on the PUPnet as wanted fugitives, we've just docked at the top place where known fugitives hide and I'm pretty damn sure we're about to do something illegal."

"You're right about one thing...we're going to do something very illegal, but if it works, then we will be in the clear and ready to go for the rest of our lives. No more BCS, no more government and we can set up wherever we want. Live out our days happy and —"

"Save the lies for your bed partner. Just tell us the plan." Frankie was the one with this gem. Sure, she was pissed because Al had chosen someone else over her, but Al really hoped she would have toughened up by now. They had never been exclusive, never been anything. Though Frankie always tended to get territorial about things.

"Fine, no stories, just plan. We are going to infiltrate an APUP outpost on Callisto. Get access to the computer and let Loyda work her magic. While that happens, Mangle and Frankie will stay with the ship. Work to make sure we are ready to take off and resupply. Sell whatever of the powder you must. At this point it doesn't matter."

Duffy scoffed. "Once you go off the deep end, you really don't dial back. I hope this space bait is worth all the trouble. Women are bad luck in space."

"Really, Duff?" Frankie slapped him on the shoulder. "Women are bad luck? I'm a woman."

"No, you're not, you're Frankie." Mangle supplied this gem. *Bunch of idiots, the whole group of them.* But they were Al's idiots.

"Is everyone good with this?"

Mangle stepped forward, his hand resting on his holstered gun. "I'm afraid I'm not."

Of course, the bastard won't quit. Al had silently wished his first mate would finally see his way. They'd traveled together for years, bonded over time spent in engineering as gophers, then as processors scrubbing their skin raw to get rid of the smell of burning flesh. Instead, they'd grown apart. *Unexpected, really.*

Loyda entered the room, fully dressed, every inch of skin covered—much to Al's disappointment. But she looked refreshed and ready to go. Of course, she added fuel to Mangle's fire.

"And her." Mangle pointed at the woman who seemed to be ruining Al for all others. "Duffy's right. Our run of bad luck started when she came on board."

"You believe in superstitions now."

Mangle made a face. "It's not superstitious if it's facts. We almost got killed on that last run, we nearly lost everything at Saturn and she probably has something to do with why we didn't do our usual drop at the ring jail. This whole thing is screwy. Tuatha will have our nuggets melted and cast in a personal set of silverware if we don't deliver something. And you think breaking into an outpost and logging into a computer will set us free?"

Al stood, ready to jump in, but Mangle shook his head. "No, don't speak, because whatever you say doesn't change things. I refuse to go down. Refuse to let you give up and lose everything just like you lost Styx."

"Fine, you don't have to stay on the ship. Transfer to another vessel. Duffy can take on your duties. Bertha will work the distraction."

Mangle sighed. "You don't get it. This isn't just me this time."

Al glanced around the room, really taking in everyone's stances. Besides Loyda and himself, everyone stood armed to the teeth, weapons either on their person or within reach. "So, you're done with us then."

"No, we took a page out of your book." Frankie stepped forward and grabbed the handle of an emergency exit that opened to a back route at the rear of the ship. "We made a deal."

As soon as the hatch opened, APUPs stormed through that entrance and others, surrounding them in record time.

"Even better."

"Betrayed. No surprise there." Loyda's last words rushed out of her as she was slammed from behind and down over the center eating table of the galley. She heard more than saw Al struggle as some spacehole pup cuffed her. When they dragged her to a standing position, another pup slammed the butt of a gun into Al's cheek.

"Al, stop struggling."

Surprisingly, he stopped. After last night, she wasn't exactly sure where things stood between them. Their core beliefs being at different ends of the spectrum made it seem even crazier that they had somehow come together and been more than perfect in that one area of things.

They slapped the cuffs on Al, and though he wasn't in a prone position, she could tell he was watching for a mistake, for a way to turn the tables.

"What are you going to do to us? Where are you taking us?" Loyda feared the worst, being dragged straight before a tribunal in the parliament floor on

Saturn. If an ambassador was behind this, he would want her dead sooner than later.

"You're going to the outpost."

"I just did what they wanted me to do." Al had started telling another tall tale. "You ask me why a crew would turn in their captain unless they wanted to rob him blind and steal his cut from the BCS. They stowed your fugitive away."

And she should have let him go. But she found his ramble of lies almost as endearing as how he liked to make sure she ate. A giant, harmless creature, unless threatened. At least he did a good imitation of one.

"Al, shut up for once in your life."

"Pups, you should listen to me. The woman is crazy. Promised my crew whatever amount of crinkle they wanted and kidnapped our vessel. I was waiting for her to get the hell out of here, then I would contact you."

He kept going and the pups did what she expected. They cuffed everyone, the whole damn family. Soon the cacophony of voices rose to the ridiculous as each one—except for Bertha, who liked like a sad animal— all argued their version of the story. Of why they shouldn't be arrested or charged or taken in. Whatever words they want to spin, whatever story they told, it didn't make a difference. It seemed everyone thought they could bargain their way out of an arrest if they just gave up something the government wanted. Except the law didn't work like that. In her training, she'd been instructed that everyone in a situation was to be arrested, even if some were innocent. The stories and lies told were often too numerous to sort out and pups were not the trained folks from the investigative division. They were enforcers. *Better to leave the real investigative work to those hired for it.*

That was how they ended up being shoved into a cell barely the size of Al's office and the door slammed shut behind them. The cuffs at that point unlocked and the group was instructed to turn over the cuffs through the box in the wall. All things she was damn familiar with — just not from this side of the process.

By the time Mangle put his cuffs in the box, Al was already stalking toward him. "I'm going to kill you."

The first mate hesitated, as if he planned to stand his ground, but then remembered he had no weapon when he was frantically reaching for his pistol on his hip. *No pistol. No choice. Completely screwed.* So he ran. In circles. The hilarity of the moment seemed to lighten the mood in the small room. Everyone else sat on benches with plenty of space between them. Loyda positioned herself in the back corner — walls on two sides made it better to defend herself. She'd seen how some folks got, being in a locked cage. They tended to lose it. She hoped this group had more experience with such things and wouldn't go bonkers.

Al never caught Mangle. No, they chased each other around for what seemed like a half a solar hour. When they slowed down, both men breathing hard, Loyda spoke. "That's why you never make a deal. Because pups are trained to not follow through on deals made with anyone."

"Unless you have the flash to pay them off," Al added. He took a seat next to her.

"We need a new plan, maybe two of them."

Al bumped her shoulder with his. "But we made it where we wanted to."

"Yes, but a little more restricted than I'd planned."

Frankie growled. "Enough with the whispering. Care to share with the rest of us? That's what brought this on to begin with. Duffy, Bertha and I don't trust her, Al. We trusted you and she's got you all screwed up."

Goddess, how she wanted to call Frankie a relentless bitch, but this wasn't a fight she'd win. Everyone in this room had more history with one another than she probably had with anything. Also, she wanted Al to defend her. Stick up for what they did share. *Which isn't more than a bed.*

"We're working on a plan to get the hell out of here, Frankie. And if you trusted me so much, then it shouldn't have wavered just because I chose to spend time with an attractive woman. Doesn't mean anything."

Mangle barked out a laugh. "Really? What about 'we help Loyda do whatever she needs to'?"

"Yeah, I can make those recommendations and still be trustworthy, dumbass."

Mangle stood from his spot next to Duffy and started to walk toward the middle of the cell, not more than a few steps. "Like I said on the ship, your stories, the lies, the plan… I don't want anything to do with it."

Enough of this shit. Al slammed a hand down on the bench beneath him. "Then don't. You're free to disappear after we escape the outpost. Go where you want and don't bother sticking around. Al and I can manage on our own without your help."

"Al and I?" Duffy pointed at Al. "You believe him, that he'll do what for you? Help you? Al is only after one thing…whatever Al can get. His interests were always a benefit to us. Now they aren't. One day, you will no longer benefit him…then it's bye-bye."

She glanced at Al, who rolled his eyes and sat up a little straighter, clasping one of her hands in his.

"Everyone seems to forget you betrayed me, not the other way around. Regardless, we have to work together to get out of here."

Right as the last word left his mouth, a group of three pups came down the hallway to their cell. The door was uncharged and opened, and guns were trained on all parties.

"Duffy, engineer. Bertha, ship's cook. Frankie, pilot. And Mangle, ship's officer. You're all free to go. Exit quickly and move out through the front of the building."

Loyda tried to prevent her mouth from dropping open. There was no way these people would be released, not without some sort of major intervention. She'd seen the processes in place, executed them a few times herself. *Impossible.* Al jumped to a standing position and Loyda heard the unmistakable click of a plasma pistol powering up.

"Al—"

"When will we be released? This is obviously a false arrest."

"Alexander Smith." Frankie walked over to him and trailed a few fingers up his fully covered arm. "To think we spent so much time together and you'd throw it all away."

Loyda growled low. She itched to punch the grin off that woman's face.

"It's time to say goodbye, Frankie."

"Goodbye, Frankie." Al's words were completely dull, lifeless, but that didn't stop Frankie from grabbing Al by the shoulder and yanking him downward so her lips could meet his.

Al tried to pull away, but the petite woman had a hell of a grip. Loyda saw her tongue slip in, and when

Frankie finally let go, Al smacked his lips together. "Goodbye, Frankie."

The woman gave Loyda a smirk and every annoying piece of her marched out of the door. The clanging slam of it sealing back in place and the charge of the electricity arcing as it charged the bars again put some finality on the situation.

"She was desperate," Loyda offered as Al sat back down, not willing to voice her jealousy or try to overpower the moment Frankie had given him. He didn't seem enthused by it, but not completely disgusted either. "You okay?"

"Yeah, let's work on that plan. We stay here too long and we might not get out."

He had a good point and time was short.

Stuck in a damn cell, hauled away—this wasn't how Al had planned for this day to end. Add on the annoyance of Loyda's lack of reaction to Frankie kissing him and he could've doubled down on getting screwed over today.

"You know…" Al brought a hand up to his mouth, careful to extract with a single finger the lockpick Frankie had transferred to him. *Make it look like you're scratching your face.* "I've lost everything since I brought you on board my ship. That piece of information I imparted to the guards was dead accurate. Nearly my life, my ship, my payload, my arrangement for a job-free future and my crew."

She scowled at him. "I didn't get the impression you cared so much about all that stuff."

"Oh, Mangle was right. I do care about how a situation benefits me." He motioned to the walls around them. "This is no benefit."

"I'm sure you'll get out of here eventually and even get back to your lovey-eyed Frankie. For now, I say you stuff it, unless you have something to contribute to a conversation that involves us busting out of here."

Guess I only needed to wait a couple more minutes. Pride swelled through him at the idea of Frankie's kiss getting Loyda's blood boiling. Al turned his bulk so his back blocked the camera's view of Loyda, then flashed the pick at her. "Jealous, huh?"

"The only thing I'm jealous of is how easily she walked out of here."

He closed the distance between them. They needed a distraction and their bickering wouldn't be enough. He leaned down, hovering next to her ear. "She means nothing, but the pick she gave me helps us. It's a weapon. We need someone in this cell. What do you suggest will get them in here, because I have a few ideas?"

Loyda turned her head, her breath hot against his neck, and she bit him. "They won't permit fornication. At least I don't think they will."

She licked the spot where she'd bitten and dragged her tongue up and around the shell of his ear. His dick went immediately rock-hard. Crazy, that was what she made him, whereas Frankie's actions did nothing. It was scary, the idea of how much power Loyda had over him, how she could send his sexual energy and adrenaline spiking with little effort. And it was funny how he'd had the same idea for a distraction too. Wrapping an arm around her waist, he lifted her and hauled her against him, grinding his pants-covered dick against her core.

"You feel so damn good." Loyda moaned the last word.

He didn't get a chance to respond before her lips were on his, taking back control.

Though clothes were still a barrier, that didn't make the feeling any less amazing — their bodies in close contact, her tongue working its own escape plan against his. It wouldn't take much to get pants down to ankles, to drive into her. Chase away some of the crap this day had delivered.

"Step back."

Right on time. Reluctantly, Al loosened his hold on Loyda, and she slid down the length of his body until her feet touched the floor. She hugged him close.

The electric grid on the doors powered down. He heard the door open, his back to the action.

"Miles, you're disgusting. Can't believe you'd let this space trash touch you. He's a Mars bastard, and you're from Saturn. Makes me sick, but I'll have to separate you if you keep it up."

"Oh, you will have to separate us, because I plan to screw her senseless right here on the cell floor. You know us Mars folk don't keep screwing to ourselves. We like audiences." Al turned around to see exactly what he was up against. The pup that had come in was half his size, wielding a plasma rifle. The wonder of government funding meant much better weapons than the gunpowder-ancient technological bullshit most of *them* had. The guard carried a big knife too.

"Shut your mouth, body collector."

"Really? That's all anyone keeps telling me. Shut your mouth…funny no one has the nuggets to try and shut it for me."

The guard growled and stalked toward Al, gun pointed at his chest. "I'll shut you up right now."

Al let go of Loyda, crouched low and charged, taking the damn fool off his feet and plowing him into the ground. The hard floor beneath them knocked the wind out of the guard with a loud gasp. Al pried the gun away from him and gave the spacehole a punch in the face for all the bullshit.

He freed the knife and tossed it towards Loyda. "Follow me."

"But I'll go—"

"You've called the shots long enough, and I can't say they got us very far. So, follow me."

The alarms sounded, and they scrambled out through the door right before the auto control shut it and the electric grid came back online. Al dashed down the hall, looking for a place to hide. He tried a few panels, pressing buttons, and had no luck with the hatches opening. Finally, one opened…to reveal a janitor's closet.

"Get inside."

"Are you serious? We need to move—they'll be searching everywhere."

Al shoved her by the shoulder into the room. He followed her, pressed the button to close the damn door, then faced her and began to whisper. "Yes, but we can let them run for the cell and try to stop us there, and sneak past a few of them. This gun, while state of the art, doesn't have infinite shots. You only have a knife."

"I would have been able to get a gun from one of the guards you shot," she hissed.

"Be quiet. We need to listen." Solar minutes ticked by, but no loud voice, no boots to the ground came. Finally, Al opened the door and peeked out. "Nothing. Shit."

They scrambled out of there and up a set of stairs to the second floor. No one, no bodies. Nothing. Everyone was gone, the alarms still rambled on and the red flashing lights above panels every few feet blinked. They got to the third floor, the main floor. Al stopped next to a group of desks and peered around a corner. A group of pups were working their way to the exit.

"Everyone's leaving for some reason."

"Maybe someone accidentally pulled a fire alarm or something."

He turned to see Loyda grabbing a data drive from its hiding spot in her boot. She tossed it into the air and grabbed it with her other hand. "Their loss, our gain. Let's do this."

Chapter Sixteen

The fact that all the pups were clearing out made her nervous. Evacuations of APU facilities never came lightly, but Loyda refused to not take a chance with this opportunity, the only shot she had to gain access to the information. This time she led, working across the main floor to one of the offices with a hardwired holo-screen and computer. Tech like this only existed in government hands, and she typed in her log-in information.

The computer *bleep boop*ed at her. The damn thing wouldn't give her access.

"Don't think those old access codes you had will work anymore, space bunny. You're a fugitive."

She tried to remember her boss's, something to do with his daughter's name and his favorite color. It took five tries, but she got in. "Keep a look out. I'll need a few minutes."

"Look out, hell. I'm going to find more weapons. What floor is the cache on?"

Her fingers flew over the keyboard, seeking access to the files she needed to prove her theory. Multi-tasking was hard. "There should be a small one behind the main desk, another one floor down. We shouldn't split up, though."

"We need to for the moment if you plan on getting out of here without some serous plasma burns. Plus, I need to find out where my ship is at. That console won't tell me."

"How do you know that?"

"I'm a body collector—I'm not stupid. They store all the information across multiple computers, to reduce the risk of being hacked. The future learned from the past. Now hurry up. I'll be back." Then Al disappeared through the door.

Loyda kept working and finally she found what she wanted. Ambassador Anu and his ship's identification matched the codes and symbols of the ship that had come to the jail before them. The only problem was that the ambassador was a huge supporter of rehabilitation for those who committed crimes, not complete disposal. She dug deeper, into his friends, allies, his wife…Tuatha.

Things started to click. She vaguely remembered the woman—elusive, a member of parliament who often avoided appearing. And the mastermind behind the deaths of thousands of people for no reason. Then she found the files on patents for a new fuel source. Not bone based, but an ore found on other planets, one with the potential to double power output in smaller amounts. Additional reports mentioned testing failure. Coupled with recordings of documented interviews with Ambassador Tuatha, and her promises to parliament that change was coming. A change to power the entire APU fleet. The proof sat at Loyda's fingertips.

"She's killing people for fuel."

"What are you mumbling to yourself?" Al walked back into the room. It couldn't have been more than five solar minutes since he'd left—at least it seemed like it.

Loyda lifted her head, ready to repeat what she now believed as fact, then caught sight of a familiar face. "What the hell is she doing here?"

"Jeez, that's the thanks I get for helping you both out of the cage." Frankie leaned against the doorway and moved a tuft of her red hair out of her face.

Al came farther into the room and tossed a gun toward Loyda. "I found her, searching for weapons. She was sitting there right on the other side of the main desk. Helped me look up where the ship is. It's impounded, so we need something else, but in the meantime, Frankie can help us."

The damn one-eyed pilot wasn't help, but trouble. Her sticking around rubbed Loyda in all the wrong ways. She finished loading the files onto the disk drive. After the proper downloads were complete, she stuck the damn thing back in her boot, then messed with the gun. Another plasma pistol, but with only half a cartridge of fuel.

"Hey, who the hell do you think pulled the alarm that got those pups out of this place? Me. I gave Al the lock pick." Frankie sounded all sorts of put out with her little 'trying to be helpful' act.

"I don't buy it." Loyda shoved herself out of the chair and walked around Al, who was still checking the additional pistols and two rifles he'd grabbed. "You betrayed him. Me. I don't know what your agenda is, but I don't trust you."

"You don't have to, because he does," Frankie pointed at Al and Loyda followed her finger's direction, looked at the man she'd come to rely on and was still relying on when everyone, even the woman standing next to her, chose to ditch him.

"Give her one more shot, Loyda. At best, she's an extra body for the pups to shoot at."

"Hey—"

Al shrugged. "It's true, and at worst, you might try to pull some shit. Sorry, Frankie, my trust lasts if you can continue to prove yourself. Crap you pulled on the ship, agreeing to Mangle's dumbass plan? I can't ignore it completely. Are we ready to move?"

Loyda shook her head. "I don't like it, but whatever. I go behind her—she can go first."

Al chuckled, relaxing his grip on the two rifles strapped to him. "Whatever powers your slip drive."

He grabbed another pistol from his belt and handed it to Frankie, who grinned up at him like a woman being given a fancy piece of jewelry. It grated on Loyda that Al's mind was focused on the wrong goals and allowing the worship of a one-eyed crazy woman to be a part of their end game.

As she walked towards the pair, Loyda decided that she'd shoot Frankie if the woman didn't prove to be a help to them. The visceral thought jarred her. She'd never been able to reconcile murdering another being before, but the idea that this woman could get Al hurt, preventing Loyda from clearing their names and stopping Tuatha, was unacceptable.

"What are you going to do besides provide distractions? Acheron is impounded—how do we get a ship?"

Frankie grinned, "Puppy, sweetheart... I can fly anything. Just get the codes to a pup shuttle, unlock it and we are cruising without any risk of being caught. It's a perfect plan. We've got the firepower to break through gates. The moon stoners, they sell masking software to block out signals and getting rid of trackers is a Mars specialty."

"You've got it all figured out, but I don't have access to the codes."

The women continued on. Al's attention moved to the APUP computer, to the holo- screen still unlocked and waiting for a search. He could easily erase everything about his past, his contract with the BSC, his very existence, and become a clean slate. The information and the Delete button were beneath his fingertips. A temptation he had never experienced coursed through his veins, the idea he could become nobody and disappear. Even travel to that haven for misfits that the nightclub owner Sweet had created out near Earth. *No more conflict, no more Tuatha, no more dead bodies.*

He typed his name, the droning of voices of the ladies in debate telling him everything was all right.

"Fine, we try it, but, Frankie, it's not a good —"

Plasma fire ripped between the two women and they both ducked to the floor. The guard Al had knocked out was standing half a room away, gun in hand, priming for a second shot, with two more flanking him. They were in for a fight.

Al pressed Delete, watched the information disappear then trained his rifle out of the door. "Heads up, ladies!"

The fire of the weapon was a bit more than he expected. But it did the necessary work, sending the guards running as plasma fire rained down building materials from the ceiling above. Loyda and Frankie jumped up and started scrambling, taking a page out of Al's book and aiming above the guards to create debris and plenty of room for the guards to be too busy trying to move to safety rather than firing at them. The plan worked, and all three of them were out of the front door and into the busy streets of Arcas on Callisto with little struggle.

The crowds gave them cover, enough to slip in and around the groups of people walking to and from clubs and the entertainment district. Sirens sounded, most likely backup from neighboring outposts in other cities.

Loyda and Frankie led the way, crisscrossing through groups of people, working their way towards the Arcas docks and their chance off the moon. Time was short before the entire outpost started hunting them.

They made it, though, without a tail and Frankie was the one to spot the pup shuttle first. No one around, nothing. *A perfect opportunity.*

"Do you have the code?" Al asked Loyda.

She shuffled along, slowing down to keep pace next to him, though one of his steps equaled two of hers. "Yes, I believe so. Codes aren't changed on ships or shuttles that frequently. And their scanners are not always updated, so we'll give it a whirl."

Both she and Frankie approached. Al kept looking out, his gun down low and trying to act relaxed when he was anything but. Heart racing, breath a little more elevated than he liked—it was hard to play the cool, nonchalant guy waiting for his ride.

"Al," Loyda hissed. "We got it, come on."

He moved toward the entry hatch of the shuttle and let out a low whistle. "Impressive."

The engine fired up, Frankie already in the pilot seat. He climbed on board. "You two make quite the pair of thieves."

"I don't plan on being in the business of thieving forever, unlike some people," Loyda replied with arms crossed.

Al tried not to be offended, but he was. Loyda made it sound like his job, what he did, was so awful, when he was far less threatening than the evil woman who had blackmailed him. A woman who had murdered hundreds and used him to retrieve the bodies.

"This shuttle is going to be tracked. I thought I could disable the tracker, but I can't." Frankie — of course — announced this right after they took off, leaving no chance for them to locate another shuttle or to buy passage on another vessel — not that he had any way to purchase passage.

"You should have disabled it before takeoff or told us before." Loyda spoke the words on his mind.

"We just have to find another way off the station."

Al growled. "That's all fine and dandy, but we need crinkle in order to get passage. We're fugitives."

"I'm sure we can come up with something." Loyda reached out and put a hand on Al's shoulder. The close contact reassured him, got his blood pumping again. For all the mess they'd gone through, a part of him wanted to believe her hand on him meant he wasn't in this alone, that she still cared on some level.

Which was why a seed of guilt formed in his gut. They had been in this whole thing together, under threat together…until he'd pushed that button that had erased him and his DNA from all APUP networks. They wouldn't be coming after him anymore.

Landing on the station was a cakewalk—they docked wherever they wanted, and it was approved.

Frankie chuckled as she finalized the docking process. "There are some perks to flying for the government. Too bad I have no interest in being controlled by them."

"All right, how do we get on another ship?" Loyda's question was met with a grin from Frankie, one that always got a good pile of space hunk moving around his veins. Bad shit happened when Frankie started smiling.

"I've got credits. Government issue, since I was so helpful turning your woman in." Frankie nodded to Loyda, who looked a little like she wanted to kill the woman.

Al wanted to do something, but focused on trying to think straight. "What do you want for them?"

"You know what I want. You, me, the skies and no more of this bitch." She trained her gun on Loyda. The gun he'd fatching given her. His chest grew tight, as if Frankie had already fired the gun at him. No way would anything happen to Loyda on his watch.

He held up a hand over Loyda's chest. not caring what she thought about his protective action. He needed to do this. "You got it, babe. Let's make the call."

"Call who?"

"Emilio and Toni. They have a ship and they know people with ships." The last people he wanted to call were his sister and her husband, but he was out of choices. He needed something. Maybe they would help, or maybe they would tell him to go to hell. Either way, it was the only option he had available to him at the moment.

"Let's do it."

Loyda covered his hand with hers. "Al, stop —"

"Loyda, seriously... let me handle this." He tried to convey with his words and his eyes that this wasn't him giving up, only another detour on this wild fatching ride they'd been on for the last solar week. Could a person fall for someone after a week? Enough to be willing to lay down their life? His mother would have said so. Looking at Loyda's frantic expression gave him the urge to erase it stronger than any pull a black hole could have.

"Fine," Loyda whispered.

"Truss her up." Frankie held out a piece of rope toward him, some crap she'd probably found up around the dash.

He cracked his knuckles and grabbed the rope. "Sure thing."

A couple of loops, some twists and he made a shitty knot, wrapped around Loyda's hands. A half-hearted attempt, to be sure, but with enough show that Frankie would hopefully believe it was secure.

She worked on making the call, while Al finished. Once done, he passed Loyda a small letter opener, some sharp antique from the damn pup's desk that he'd shoved into his boot for extra protection in case he needed it. He wanted to kiss her, but heard the connection go through on the holo-screen.

"Identify yourself, government shuttle." Toni's voice was unmistakable. He'd been listening to it ever since he was five years old.

He didn't give Frankie a chance to speak, moving forward and sliding into the passenger seat. "Well, hello, little sister. You're looking good."

"Al, what the hell? Thought you said I was dead to you, never speaking to me again?"

He shrugged. "Call this a truce of sorts. I find myself in an awkward situation and I need a ship."

"And my wife needs an apology." The image of Emilio Morales, the giant scar on his left cheek a clear reminder of the gang past he'd come from, filled the screen, blocking Al's view of Toni.

"I'm not calling to play kiss and make up. I'm calling because I have a business proposal."

Toni pushed her arm around Emilio and started shoving him to the side. "What...ugh, Emilio, quit with the protective crap and move. Let me handle this or I swear I'll taser you."

Al almost laughed. The way his sister grew impatient, how Emilio did exactly what his sister said, though he didn't move far enough away... Al could still see him, arms crossed, glowering at the screen. It reminded him of the domestic moments he and Loyda had shared. What he wouldn't give—

"Spit it out, Al. The longer this connection stays, the more likely we'll get traced or worse."

He nodded. "Right, as I said we need—"

"A ship, and we have her to trade." Frankie reached back and pulled Loyda forward by the hair. Al wanted to stop her, almost smacked Frankie's face, but held himself still.

Playing the game ensured they didn't get into a gunfight. They couldn't afford attention or to draw the pups to them.

"Loyda Miles. I'll be... Shit, Emilio, it's the investigator who helped Sweet and Rina. And she's wanted by everyone in parliament right now."

Al's interest perked at that. "What do you mean?"

"Untold rewards are what they're promising. She knows something, if parliament wants her that bad. They're desperate." Toni shared a look with Emilio, one that told Al there were wheels turning, plans in motion, and he wouldn't be able to stop them. Not if he wanted to get them the hell out of there.

"We'll help," Emilio chimed in. "Transportation from wherever you are, in exchange for Loyda."

His fight-or-flight response roared, the *No* louder than a sonic wave. He wanted to scream it. To grab Loyda, to hide her—anything rather than turning her over to be used by someone else. Frankie waved the barrel of her gun at Loyda, the motion catching his eye. Loyda wasn't safe here or, for that matter, anywhere. But with Toni and Emilio, she would get another chance to escape. Al would make sure of it.

"We have a deal. How soon can you get to Callisto space station?"

Chapter Seventeen

Emilio and Toni wouldn't make it in time, at least not fast enough. The pup shuttle would be a magnet, so Toni told them to go to some woman's shop. Loyda didn't remember the name, because she was still in shock. A deep-seated feeling of futility had snagged her when the guards had started shooting at her in the outpost. How much more running would she have to do? How long before they caught up to her and there was no chance to get her story out? She needed time, and that seemed to be the very thing she didn't have.

Frankie was determined to kill her. She could see it in the woman's eyes now, a cold-blooded, jealous gleam that overrode any other emotion the woman possessed. "Why do they want her? We could easily end her, claim the reward. I'm sure they'd give something to have the body back. You know how it is — bodies are worth almost the same as alive."

"Shut up, Frankie," Al said, and kept walking. The crowds on Callisto station were almost as numerous as they were on the streets of Arcas. People milled around—vendors, ships seeking passengers, flash exchanges, restaurants, black market dealers who traded all sorts of illegal activity. Either way, for the moment, they fitted in. No one cared that they had guns, because half the people here had them.

Al kept Loyda tucked against his side, an arm around her. Her hands were still bound, with a jacket laid over them to hide the fact. She hated it, wanted to voice her opposition, but she couldn't tell what side Al was on. One minute he'd said her name, cracked his knuckles, then he'd tied her hands up. Sure, the knot itself wasn't crazy and she had the knife, tucked between her palms, but it didn't stop her from wishing she could ask Al what the hell he was thinking, the plan he had.

At that exact moment, Al squeezed her arm. She glanced up, but he wasn't looking at her. No, he navigated them through the small clusters of people, two ladies haggling over the price of a dress and a pair of idiots betting on a shell game.

None of it stopped her thoughts from running in a million directions. Who could she truly trust? What did Emilio and Toni want with her? Her experience with them was limited—she'd dealt with Sweet and Rina, who were awesome people. Emilio and Toni were outlaws, more so than Al had ever been. These were people who wanted her holo-recordings as much as she did. They could be working for Tuatha and Frankie could decide to kill her at any moment.

Loyda needed to run. Run and make her own damn way. *Somehow.* But whatever she felt towards Al couldn't be trusted either. Love wasn't an emotion that led people to make good choices. At least that was what she'd seen from experience, from her parents' marriage. Love grew from respect and admiration—outside Al's sheer strength and his prowess in the bedroom, what did she admire?

A gunshot rang out and Loyda waited for the pain, the agony to overtake her body. Instead, Al pushed into her, moving her to the left, down a side passage, away from the main street. This was her chance. They came to a stop and he put himself in front of her, to protect her.

"Stay still." Al's pulse was racing—she could tell by the way he breathed, short and fast. His heat warmed her. *Goddess, I'll miss this.*

"What's happening?" Loyda worked with the knife to get her bonds free. It didn't take much.

Frankie's boots clacked toward them. "Come on, Al. Danger's passed. Some idiot shot someone else over refusal to refund part of his passage fee. We got to move."

Al stepped back, opening his mouth to say something and Loyda decided it was now or never. Hunching low, she shoved into Al's gut, forcing him to move backward a couple of steps. She dropped the jacket, the knife, everything, in her urgency to run. Something near the wall, a pipe or who knew what, tripped up her left foot and she stumbled.

Regaining her balance took a couple of wobbly steps and she heard the whine of a plasma pistol charge. She could dodge and weave, but the alleyway ahead of her, though dark, didn't provide enough space to create a wide field of fire. There was a good chance, no matter what, that she'd get hit, so she went for the next best thing. Dropping to the ground.

Again, she prepared for pain, waited to hear the burst of fire come shooting out of the barrel. Her vision focused on the darkness ahead, her hands and feet poised to propel her upwards. To launch forward and run again if she got lucky.

Except the shot never came. Instead there was a clatter, a guttural word, a choke.

Loyda got up and turned around, ready for the worst, another enemy. Instead it was Al. Standing there, Frankie on the ground with blood surrounding her. The knife in Al's hand told the story, but she wanted to hear him say it.

"Al, what happened?"

"I killed her."

Al killed people. It had happened over the years. The list wasn't huge, but it wasn't short. Somewhere in between a big number and a little one. Frankie on the ground in front of him had represented the first time he'd killed someone who'd been a friend to him, shared his bed and at one time had known him better than anyone else. Except she'd betrayed him.

They all do in the end.

Right, that was what would happen. Except he couldn't feel sorry for it. No matter how hard he tried to summon sympathy, Frankie had lost it the moment she'd turned that gun on Loyda. The woman had always hated losing, but killing someone over a loss was pointless to Al.

"Al, we can't stay here." Loyda's voice broke through the fog of staring at Frankie's eyepatch, her face frozen in shock.

"Yeah, I know. The place we need to go is down this hallway." They'd been so close. Close to getting the hell out of there. *Zentha's Wild Rides*, the sign blinked in a low-level blue light. Anyone not knowing where they hell they were going would have missed it.

"I don't understand what happened."

Al groaned. "I think it's kind of obvious — she was going to kill you."

"You didn't have to try and stop her."

This woman drove him absolutely crazy. "Yeah, I did."

They reached the entrance to the place. Toni had been right — it looked shady as hell. He banged on the metal roll-down hatch. Hopefully this Zentha lady would be here.

"Why, Al?"

He didn't answer and banged his fist on the metal door again. His feelings for her were super confusing, too much to unravel at the moment. Besides, it was the wrong time to say what he wanted to. A horrible time to do anything but get moving.

"Al, talk to me." She grabbed his arm, forcing him to look at her.

It was the hardest damn thing he had to do, because she wanted answers. She looked at him with all sorts of questions in her eyes.

"You don't want to ask the questions and I don't want to answer what you won't ask. Let's leave it at that."

The door to Zentha's flew open right then. *Perfect damn timing.*

"What do you want?" The woman posing the question stood as tall as Al. He almost asked if they were related, expect where his hair was red, hers was as white as cocaine.

"E and T said that you could provide a shuttle and charge the fee to them. They will have it back to you in two solar weeks." *Here's hoping my sister's instructions held up and they paid this woman enough to do their dirty work.*

The woman let out a sigh. "Fine, I'll do it, but you tell them when you see them that just because they got my daughter out of that cartel harem doesn't mean they get transportation needs for anyone they want. I have a business to run."

Al almost told the lady to forget it. This whole thing was crap. They would find another way, except Loyda spoke instead. "Fine, happy to let them know. And we appreciate your help this one time."

A commotion of people grew at the end of the passage. Frankie's body had been found.

"Could we step inside?"

Zentha peered around the wall, glancing down the way they'd come. "If they ask me about the body, I'll have to tell them about you. I won't lie."

"We're not asking you to," Loyda replied.

The woman stepped to the side and let them pass. Al went along with it, still warring with himself, with what he'd done. In fact, he barely paid attention the entire time Zentha talked them through the shuttle. It was like most of the shuttles he'd seen, with a few extra add-ons. Loyda did most of the talking, Al playing strong and silent. They got off the station and out into space without pups barging in, weapons primed. Without an explosion or threats or the need for guns. Within minutes they were that much closer to the rendezvous point somewhere near the asteroid belt, engaging the slipstream drive and plugging in autopilot. That was when Loyda undid her seat belt and turned to face him.

Al kept looking forward. Leaving control of piloting to a computer system seemed risky when floating through a wide path of sharp-edged rocks with steam-filled centers. He wasn't sure whether he was hurtling forward or backward, but he didn't like any of it.

"Why did you kill her, Al?"

"Looking for a motive to go with my murder confession on the station, Investigator?" Because if she wanted to see him jailed for the rest of his life, he'd already given her the weapon to do so. So much for his freedom that he'd earned with a delete button. It would be gone in a heartbeat.

"No, that's not why I want to know."

Al's chest grew tight. "You're not asking the right question, then."

"What's the right question?"

For some reason the air had thinned, the cabin of the shuttle growing warm, which wasn't supposed to happen in space. "We sure this death trap is in proper working order?"

"Zentha went through the pre-flight sequence with us both. Everything checked out. Now quit trying to change the subject and talk to me."

"I had to kill her. That's the best way I can explain it, the only way. Leave it at that."

"Are you sad?"

Al tugged at his beard. The ends needed trimming, as he gathered from a simple touch, and it made him mad. "That's the worst part, no. I'm not sad… I'm fatching relieved. Is that awful or what? I'm thankful I kept you safe, but I have no clue what to do with that."

Loyda rose from her seat and crossed the small distance between them. Standing in front of him, she undid his seatbelt. "Come with me."

"Someone has to keep an eye out."

She grabbed both his arms and tugged. "We're cloaked. That's the type of shuttle she gave us, one designed for stealth. We'll know someone is there before they even know we exist. There's hours left until we hit the asteroid belt, and a few more until Emilio's ship gets there."

How could he argue with that? He stood up and followed her to the back half of the shuttle, where a wide bunk, big enough that at least one of them could lie down, was built into the wall. "You want me to tuck you in?"

"You idiot man. No, I want you to lie down and let me do what I need to."

Al closed his eyes and took a deep breath, summoning what little resolve he had left. "Loyda, we shouldn't—"

Her lips closed over his, and she stuck her tongue out, taking full advantage of his partially opened mouth. Damn if she wasn't the hottest thing he'd ever had in his life. The objections died there. God he'd want her anytime, anywhere, for the rest of his days.

The truth slapped him in the face. He pulled back, took in her panting breaths, her heaving chest, the breasts confined by her clothing that he could remove in under a minute. This was good between them. She was amazing, brave... "She almost killed you, would have killed you."

"But she didn't. You saved me. I'm right here and asking you to please remind me how alive I am."

"You ask and you shall receive." He picked her up and took her to the bunk.

Al stripped her of every stitch of clothing, then stripped himself. From there, it didn't take much, but he touched her slowly, watched her every reaction to what he did, and now he knew her body. Anticipated what she liked, how she liked it, and how long it took for her to orgasm.

Seeing her in the throes of release made everything that much better and worse. Because he knew then, as he pushed inside her, feeling her heat clasp his dick like a docking clamp on a tether, that he loved her. More than anything, anyone. He'd kill for her, commit numerous crimes in her name. Whatever she asked, he would give himself up to please her, and that was scarier than any gun he'd faced down, any dangerous mission in open space. This woman held all the power and, for all he knew, she tolerated him because he was damn good in bed.

Which was what he focused on, let wash over him. The desire to please her, to chase her pleasure with his as he pounded into her again and again. Then he flipped positions.

"Your turn. Make yourself come alive and use me to do it." He guided her with his hands on her hips, up and down. He clasped her hand and brought it to her center, covering her fingers with his and directing her to stroke that nub between her legs.

The final piece of the puzzle was to lean up and clasp his mouth over one of her nipples. She screamed and he loved it. He worried, bit and teased that nipple over and over until she yelled out his name, her channel hot and gripping as her release washed over her.

Al took control then, using her body to finish himself off and wringing additional moans of pleasure from her lips. "I'm going to come."

Except she didn't leave him. No, she let his hot seed spill into her, and he'd never known such bliss. The only problem was that this was just the physical. The emotional aspect he couldn't confess, not if she didn't feel the same way, and asking... That was damn scary. She'd already confessed to her job being the most important thing in the world to her. No criminal would fit into that plan, especially one that no longer existed. Her future lay with the government, clearing her name to take her rightful place among the ruling class of their universe.

As he fell asleep with her body draped over him, he committed to keeping any words of love to himself, because he couldn't rely on her to return those feelings anytime soon.

Chapter Eighteen

Loyda woke to a low-toned beeping coming from the cockpit area. She held her breath, waiting for the alarms to start to ring out. Goddess knew she'd had one pitfall after another over the last week. She'd started to believe that danger truly waited for her around every corner.

She climbed off the bed and scrambled into her clothes, shivering as she went. In the heat of the moment, passion had provided plenty of warmth, but once she was no longer huddled next to the furnace Al created, she was freezing. Once clothed, she made it to the dash and shut off the alert system. The vid-screen reflected what she'd assumed—they were at the rendezvous point. All they had to do was wait.

Based on the time, it would be a matter of a couple hours until Emilio and Toni intercepted them. Loyda wasn't sure if she was ready for the next steps. She glanced back at Al, who'd started to stir. He'd awoken parts of her she hadn't been as in tune with before.

Their romp and rest afterwards held all the warning signs. She was falling for this perfectly bad, unsuitable man. Her parents would be horrified at her even voicing the ideas rattling around in her brain.

This is temporary. Yes, she had to stay focused on the end goal. Clearing her name and, by extension, her family's. A relationship was the last thing she needed or wanted, since her family had already signed her up for a future with Gaylord. *Who doesn't give a damn about me.*

She looked at Al again. His eyes were open and he was staring at her. "A star for your thoughts."

"Just thinking about last night."

Al chuckled, then stretched his arms up above him. "It wasn't as cold as it is now."

"That's for sure."

"I could warm you up." The suggestion was paired with a wink, and he almost had her saying yes. Therein lay the problem. She needed to keep things objective, be focused on the end goal. He'd provided distraction, reassurance and a chance to unwind. Long term, flights of fancy had no place in this damn shuttle.

"A nice offer, but I'd hate for your sister to show up and get a look at my bare ass."

"You're right." He sat up and moved to the edge of the bunk. "Don't need anything else to make my sister jealous."

"You sure know how to flatter a woman."

He grabbed his clothes off the floor and started to pull them on. "And I'm not even trying."

He covered up that gorgeous naked form, the skull and crossbones tattoo on his shoulder disappearing. "What's the shoulder tattoo about?"

"Family crest. People on the uppers got fancy family symbols, Loyda?"

"Yeah, though ours are more about mottos than what the crest is. Some families only have a symbol of a leaf or a raindrop, a lightning bolt or something simple."

He moved up near her, taking the passenger seat. "Motto, huh? I guess my family motto would be *Beat Them Before They Beat You.*"

Then the alarm sounded, loud blaring noise accompanied by flashing red lights and the vid-screen highlighting an incoming ship targeting them.

"What the fatch?" Al's relaxed stance immediately went tense.

It wasn't lost on Loyda that he'd recited a motto that basically called for selling people out. "They found us somehow. Someone tipped them off. Did you really kill Frankie?"

"That's your first thought, that I didn't kill my childhood friend so she could send a shuttle after us? That doesn't make any damn sense."

Loyda tried to pull up a clearer visual, but the shuttle system wasn't familiar to her. Even with Zentha's limited instructions, Loyda was at a loss. "Nothing makes sense anymore. But I didn't tell anyone where we were. Unless your sister sold us out. Doesn't she follow the same family motto?"

"Enough. The worst case, we got followed from Callisto station or they made Zentha talk."

A ring sounded over the vid-screen. They were being hailed.

Loyda let her finger hover over the accept button. "Do I answer that?"

"Keep it audio only. That way they don't know how many are on this ship." Al nodded and she pressed the button.

"Attention, vessel. We are hailing Al Smith to thank him for his help in apprehending Loyda Miles. We are happy to present our pure flash reward, along with the return of his ship Acheron. Prepare to be docked and boarded."

Before the damn traitor could respond, Loyda ended the communication. "Are you fatching kidding? We survived all of that and you're selling out? You saw what Tuatha did, claimed to hate her even more for what she did to you. The woman is pure evil, according to your words, and now I'm expendable."

Loyda started searching for a weapon, something to protect herself with. She'd lost her normal package of knives and her gun. Zentha hadn't volunteered to supply them with weapons. They weren't supposed to need any.

"Hold on there, just a solar minute." Al reached for her and she batted his hand away.

"Back the hell off before you lose a limb."

"Okay, I'm backing off, but this isn't me."

She wanted to believe it, that look of earnest pleading on his face. He kept his arms up as she darted her gaze from spot to spot, seeking something to stab him with or bash his damn head in. Everything they'd been through proved that he came from a background where telling the truth was only possible if it benefited someone.

"Loyda, look at me."

"It's too late for that... Where's your damn gun?"

No way in hell would Al give Loyda a weapon. In her current state, she might use it and damn whoever, most likely Tuatha, who decided to try to convince him to turn Loyda over. "Hold off on the trigger-happy desire and let's talk about this."

"You sold me out—there's nothing to say."

He sighed, hands still held up to show he meant to take no action. "Have you learned nothing by being around me? People will say anything to get what they want, even spin lies in the hopes it will flush out their prey."

"I can't trust that."

The shuttle rattled as the larger vessel tethered to them. He had one gun, maybe half a cartridge of plasma fluid. So, five shots maximum. There was only one way in and one way out, with one space suit in the back. Zentha, that shrewd woman, had refused to provide a second one. She had a limit to the amount of help a favor entailed.

"You can't, but there's nothing else. If we're going down, I wish you'd believe I didn't plan this."

She crossed her arms and slunk back into the captain's chair, not sparing another word for him. Everything seemed to mean nothing in the face of lies some other idiot had spewed. He wanted to fight her on the topic. Get her to see his way of things because, hell, this wasn't how he'd seen them ending.

No, he wanted to find a way for them to be together, even if it meant stolen moments on some backward moon in a small house with just the two of them every few solar months. *Whatever.* He'd be whatever she wanted, though he'd hate the idea of another man touching her. The possibilities seemed useless if she didn't trust a damn word out of his mouth.

"Well, you're not exactly trustworthy. Screw your conscience."

The shuttle hatch gave way as whoever was on the other side cut through. Al decided to stand up and face the bastards. To find out exactly who'd put him and Loyda's possible future at the entrance to a black hole.

The snobby prick who walked through the shuttle hatch was none other than Loyda's fiancé, Gaylord. "Where's Loyda?"

The woman in question, *his* woman, peeked her head around the edge of the captain's seat and stood, alarm apparent in the way she went ramrod straight.

"Gaylord, what the hell are you doing here?"

"I'm here to take you home, so we can be married."

Over my dead body. The pompous idiot wore some type of cape over his clothing, lined with the fur of an animal in an attempt to look threatening or rich. Either way, the effect was lost on Al.

"Why are you wearing a blanket?" he asked.

Gaylord didn't even look in his direction and took two steps toward Loyda. "I promised your parents I would get you out of this mess."

Loyda scrambled out of the seat, and Al didn't like the way she appeared nervous. She had nothing to be afraid of. If this idiot threatened her, Al would take him out.

"How does getting married solve my problems?"

"It doesn't, but the weight of my name being yours, of us still marrying, will show those who doubt you that you are still fit to serve in parliament."

Al started to laugh. He couldn't help it — the words coming out of this idiot's mouth were too ridiculous. "And let me guess, she'll still be convicted in front of her peers. What a joke. What part of her soul does she have to include, besides the rest of her life given to an Upper idiot like you?"

The words provoked Gaylord to turn and acknowledge Al. Of course, he had to look up, because Al was taller. There was a smidge of satisfaction at forcing this fool to lift his head to him.

"The body collector, Captain Alexander Smith, correct?"

"Interesting, you know my name."

Gaylord sniffed. "Yes, unfortunately. It will take some additional time to wipe the filth and stench of your name associated with my future bride's. Loyda, enough nonsense. Let's go. We can be back to Saturn in less than two days, married in less than three."

Al clenched his fists. All she had to say was no or give him any other sign she didn't want to leave with this would-be fiancé and he'd act. He'd take everyone out. He ignored the two guards that were positioned by the entrance, with two additional guards on the other side of the hatch. The guns were primed and ready to shoot. Gaylord…didn't appear to be armed. The plan unfolded in Al's head.

"Gaylord, I refuse to turn myself in until I have the evidence I need to prove my innocence. I'm close to getting it. Give me those three days to find what I need, and I'll meet you on Saturn."

The fiancé shook his head. "I can't, Loyda. The only way I could get your location was to promise I would bring you back to Saturn immediately."

"Who gave you the location?" Al asked, finalizing his size-up of his competition. He could take them down, he was sure of it.

Ignored again, Gaylord stepped towards Loyda. "Your family is shamed. You're chasing ghosts and being blamed for the death of thousands. You should have married me sooner. Our union will provide more protection."

"It won't. It will just put you at the mercy of someone else." Al supplied, taking a sideways step towards the guards.

"Shut up, I'm talking to my fiancée. Loyda, does this body collector really have some sort of input on your opinions or thoughts?"

Al couldn't read Loyda. Her arms and hands were hanging loose, her gaze not focused on anyone in particular, as if she were considering what her dumb fiancé had suggested.

A proximity alert sounded, and Al never heard such perfect timing. Maybe this would wake her the hell up, but Al still didn't have the answer to the question he'd asked, the answer he needed Loyda to hear. Needed because her lack of trust in him still stung.

"Gaylord, that would be our ride, so we need to hurry this along." Al moved a little closer to the guards again, closer to a gun.

"You're not going anywhere. Your people wouldn't dare attack."

"You obviously don't know my sister very well."

Right on time, as if Toni could read his damn mind, an EMP rocked both ships. The power went out.

Gaylord let out a yell. *The idiot.*

Al took it as a sign to make his move. The guard didn't take long to secure. Except the electromagnetic pulse that gave him the edge made the weapon in his hands inoperable. The damn gun was only good for bashing people over the head, which was exactly what he did. Two guards down, then he saw a spark of light.

Lee, Toni and Emilio were making their way toward the entrance connecting the two ships.

The extra help headed his way gave Al the opportunity to get to Loyda. Who stood helping Gaylord off the floor.

"Get up. You won't die because the power went out." Loyda's voice crystal clear and all business.

"I know that. We need to hide. They could be enemies of my patron."

"My parents are your patrons."

Gaylord shook his head right as the power came on. "They were, but I have a new one now. Let's leave, Loyda. We go back to Saturn and put this whole thin—"

"Too late for that, Gaylord." Al grabbed him by his fur-lined cape and yanked, and the damn thing started to rip in his hands. *So much for the quality of the uppers.* "I need to know who your patron is, and now. Or my associates back there may not let your ship go."

Gaylord peeked over his shoulder the best he could and squeaked at the sight of the people standing there. Loyda looked too, and her face didn't lighten or show any sign of excitement. Sure, his sister and Emilio had implied they might be selling her to the highest bidder, but they were a better choice than this idiot.

"So, tell me, Gaylord, who is your patron?"

"Ambassador Tuatha Anu."

The name tied everything into a bow. If anything, Loyda should have been elated. She'd believed an ambassador was behind everything from the start. Except she didn't appear happy or encouraged by the confession. She looked a little green, like she had in the processing room on the Acheron.

"You're joking." Her statement wasn't lost on Al. The words sounded as if she was defeated. As if she'd lost everything. Al could relate to that voice, the tone. He'd been there. He wanted to rush to her side. But she needed to make the choice on her own.

"What will it be, Loyda? Go with Toni and her husband or stay here with Gaylord?"

"You won't be here long after we report the ship to the collection service." Emilio added that extra bit and Gaylord shuddered.

"Loyda, we can help." This from Toni. Her voice was sympathetic, and she probably spoke from experience. His sister and her husband had spent their entire married life on the run, constantly outmaneuvering the APU.

Al wouldn't lie—if anyone asked, the next thirty seconds were the worst of his life. The idea that Loyda would give up after they'd come so far. The idea that this would be the last time he saw her. *Fatch*. He was an idiot, a tough guy turned sucker for a woman.

Loyda sighed, and it sounded bone-weary. "Gaylord, tell my mother and father I'm sorry."

Chapter Nineteen

It had been at least two solar hours since Loyda had left Gaylord on Zentha's shuttle. He'd pouted like a petulant child, a grown man acting like she'd put him out in such a way. Except his parting words had been more threat than tantrum.

"I'm not giving up on you. This arrangement is far from over. We are not done." That was the last sentence he'd yelled.

Those words replayed over and over, along with Gaylord's confession, as Loyda showered in the private quarters Emilio had walked her to. She'd been instructed to join them in the galley afterwards. Dried and dressed, she was as ready as she'd ever be to thank her rescuers.

"If only I could find the galley."

A blue light lit up along a bar that ran the length of the middle of the room. It ran through the entire ship. Then a crystal-clear female voice came. "The galley is located center ship. You can find it by going right or left, as the ship design is a circle."

"Thank you?" Loyda had no clue if she should say more. AI ships were things of fantasy. People didn't tend to buy them unless they were at the top of the upper echelons. And for her parents—though they were respected and wealthy and she'd wanted for nothing as a child—such a purchase would be unnecessary and frivolous.

"You can call me *Gina*. Your heart rate and body posture imply you are not sure how to communicate with me. Names make things easier."

Loyda chuckled. "Well. you've taken the guesswork out of it."

"I try to be helpful where I can. The crew and Captain Al are waiting for you in the galley when you are ready."

"Let them know I'm coming."

The light extinguished and Loyda walked out of the door. The ship itself was a marvel of cleanliness, a stark contrast to the Acheron or any other ship she'd been on. She had half a mind to ask how such things were possible. Ships by nature couldn't stand up against decay that happened due to the cold of space or the mess that made up humans. But this whole ship put everything else to shame.

Entering the galley, she was prepared to ask just that, but Toni headed her off. "You're ready to ask about the ship, but Gina is a mystery and I think she prefers it that way."

"I do," Gina replied, her blue light blinking along the wall.

Loyda smiled and took note of everyone in the room. She recognized most of the faces, and only because she'd had brief dealings with them almost half a solar year prior. The sound of each person's voice confirmed the recognition, from the doctor they had on board to the genius who ran their engineering and the deadly killer help. Everyone fit, like an awkward family, except for Al. His bulky frame seemed problematic almost anywhere, except on the Acheron. Here he appeared even more out of sorts.

Looking at Al, who kept his eyes on the bowl of food in front of him, made a twinge of guilt wrap around her stomach. She'd believed he'd sold her out and she'd have to make things up to him.

The best way would be to get you both out of this mess.

"I need help." All the best solutions came from a simple statement, a reasonable ask. Though what Loyda had dreamed up might not be too simple or too safe.

Emilio cleared his throat. "We gathered that from the moment you reached out to us. The question really is what kind of help are you talking about, because we can do a lot of things, but not everything."

"There's a really bad woman. Her name is Tuatha Anu. She's an ambassador and a member of the APU parliament."

Lee chuckled. "Name me an ambassador who isn't bad. That's not new news, Inspector."

Al chunked his fist against the table. "Calm the sarcasm and let her talk, assassin."

"Oh, and what will you do if I don't?"

The tension could be cut with a water torch, with all the hatred being thrown by every gaze in the room.

"Don't give me a reason to toss you out of an airlock, Smith. You're here because my wife spoke up for you. The rest of us still haven't forgiven you for the role you played in everything that got us into this mess." Emilio's voice was firm and strong, even as Toni reached for him.

Loyda found the efforts endearing but distracting. "I'd appreciate quiet until I get this all out. I've almost died three or four times... I've lost count. Give me five solar minutes to speak and you can ridicule me all you like."

The room went deathly quiet. No one said a thing, made a sound or even moved. Gina's light blinked. "Continue, Inspector Miles."

"Right. Tuatha is behind all this killing. The killings on Callisto, the spread of the drug Morales was asked to transfer, my boss's death and the disappearance of everyone at the Saturn ring jail. It's really the tip of the galaxy, though." Loyda reached into her pants pocket and pulled out the drive. "All the information about this woman, and possibly more about her activities, is on this drive. I don't have time to sift through all the information I gathered. But I believe this might provide some ammunition to bring her down."

"Excuse me, but how would we do that?" Another woman, one whom Loyda recognized as Dottie, the pilot, raised this question.

"I'm not one hundred percent sure yet, but I have some ideas. Mainly about exposing her in front of a parliament session, but that's where I need you all. I need to first make sense of this information and put enough together to prove without a shadow of a doubt that this woman is up to nefarious plots. Then I need to sneak into the main parliament hall on Saturn. It's nearly impossible to do, but this crew has done some pretty impossible things in the past."

Sampson stepped forward, pulling his beanie off to reveal a shock of red hair. "I can look at the drive. Technology is my thing."

"It really is," supplied Gina, her blue light a beacon of endorsement.

"I believe you both." Loyda extended the drive toward him. "How long will it take?"

Sampson shrugged. "If it was just me, solar days. With Gina's help, maybe a day, tops."

One problem solved. "And the other thing?" She expected Emilio and Toni to tell her no, for the entire room to riot against the idea. "I completely understand if it's a no. I wouldn't want to risk my life for something that has nothing to do with me either. It's risky, to be sure, and probably idiotic—"

"I'm the biggest idiot in the galaxy, according to any pup you talked to," Emilio said as he came toward her.

Loyda wasn't afraid as much as she was impressed. This was a man who'd survived on Earth, amongst cartels and gangs. Who'd fought his way off the surface for a better life that seemed to involve a high amount of danger. "Still, it might not be worth it."

"Toni believes it is. So does the rest of my crew, and this is the exact reason we picked you up. We want the same thing. A stop to the senseless murder of thousands. Dottie, Doc, Sampson and even Lee have lost friends to this mysterious ailment spreading through the galaxy. If you're right, and we fully believe you are, then this Tuatha is to blame. We'll help you stop her if we can."

Relief unlike any she'd ever known coursed through her veins. If Loyda hadn't been hellbent on making a tough impression, she would have sunk to the floor.

Awkwardly enough, Al moved around the center table to her side. "Need to rest?"

"No, I'm fine. I'm...finally going to make this happen."

Toni walked over to her and grinned. "Yes, you are. Now, what about you, big brother? Care to help us craft the entry plan?"

Loyda looked up at Al expectantly. She wanted him in on this. To use his genius...hell, he'd helped her figure out how to break into a pup station, though it hadn't happened as planned. He looked uninterested.

"I'm looking to get a Mars drop-off, if you can manage it before you go charging off to take on the entire system establishment."

Toni nodded.

"Al, can we talk a minute?" Loyda tugged on his arm, let go and headed for the door. She could sense him behind her, following. Neither did she miss the strange look that Toni gave them both. The woman could think whatever she wanted.

"What's up?"

As soon as she got out of the galley and into the hallway, she turned, Al right on her heels. "You can't leave yet. Your future is on the line, mine as well. Why would you give up when we're so close?"

Al ground at the floor with the toe of his grav boot. "Loyda, thing is...what I need to say. Damn it, I'm not a hero, Loyda."

She reached for him and he took a step back. "I get that, but I'm not saying you have to be a hero."

"Yeah, for this crap you do." He scrubbed his face with both hands, trailing them down and wrapping his beard around them in circles. "Fatch, this mission was never mine. Always yours. And I don't need to worry about Tuatha anymore, or anything for that matter."

Anxiety, awful like a roaring, incinerating fire, barreled through her midsection. "What do you mean?"

"I deleted my records in that damn pup station. Goodbye to the APU history of Alexander Smith. No longer a captain for the BCS or a wanted fugitive. They won't be looking for me anytime soon. BCS does yearly checks against APU info, and if there's no info, then I'm dead."

"But all your credits." The words came out hollow, and she hated each one.

"Establishment banks aren't the only place to keep flash. I've been stashing for a while."

"Then this was all to, what…get you a free pass?"

Al leaned down and looked her straight in the eyes, no blinking, no knuckle cracking. "I tagged along because I had to, then I looked for a way out. That pup outpost provided it. I told you before, Smiths are always looking for the way to benefit from the situation. Nothing more, nothing less. A hero never benefits."

Loyda reacted before she could think twice, slapping him as hard as she could, though very little satisfaction emerged even as his head rocked to the side.

"I deserved that. Except you're going on a path I can't follow." Al massaged his jaw and resisted the urge, the overwhelming desire, to pop his knuckles.

"No, you refuse to. Are you afraid?"

"A bit, but let's face it, you don't trust me. My stunt back there proved it. Your eagerness to accuse me of selling you out."

Loyda's hands went to her hips, her voice gaining volume. "You haven't given me a reason to."

Bullshit. "I killed one of my childhood friends for you. Sacrificed my future as a captain of my own vessel." He could go on and on about how he'd thrust himself head first into danger for her. Time and again, like a fool thinking with his dick. "I'm not doing it again. This isn't my battle and I don't care. I don't care if the whole universe burns because of Tuatha's little stunt. People eventually die. Bodies to dust and fuel is where we're all headed, but I made it. I have a chance of a future that I want, away from the trouble life in space brings. I'm going to settle somewhere and be happy."

"What the hell are you talking about? It will eventually catch up to you."

Al shook his head. "Nope, I'll be sipping delicious water on a beach somewhere. Who knows, maybe that new planet, Eden, has a spot for me. I'll go home first, cobble together a ship, retrieve my crinkle and start over. The contract, my bad misdeeds and my parentage are gone forever. If you weren't so hellbent on being a hero, you could join me."

Loyda looked at him like he'd lost it, and Al already knew they'd attracted attention. That at least two or more of his sister's crew were listening to every word they said, and he'd added to his bad reputation. *So put the urine on the bone powder.* "You know where all this is leading. You know what happened to those bodies, to everyone in that jail. We can't change that."

"But we could stop it from happening again."

Al rolled his eyes and groaned. "Can you? Bad people come and go, new ones take their place. Even Lee, a natural-born killer, can see that as plain as the piercing in my nose. The government will always be corrupt. Fighting on the side of the pups doesn't change those laws, just reinforces them.

"And you say you don't care."

All in all, a part of him did care. It hurt for those who'd lost their lives in this fight and the many more who would. Putting himself on the line didn't seem to really influence things one way or another. So he sucked up his urge to say Loyda's name, to crack his knuckles again, and prepared to lie. "I don't care about them. I don't care about you and I'm done."

Then he turned on his heel, ignoring the shocked look on his sister's face and the scowling one on Emilio's, and walked away.

Chapter Twenty

Three solar days. That was how long it'd been since Al had exited Gina's loading platform and disappeared amid the Mars dust.

Loyda wanted to say she didn't miss, didn't think about him, but if anyone had asked, she wouldn't have been able to lie. She wanted Al back almost as much as she enjoyed breathing—which was ridiculous, because he would be the last choice she'd ever have made for herself. The last guy she would have thought about giving her heart to. And yet her heart was stupid.

"I think I've got most of the video pulled together, all the data in order like we discussed." Sampson's voice dragged her out of her musings. She needed to focus on the task at hand and get things wrapped. They'd holed up on Sweet's planet, Eden, since leaving Mars—a perfect place to hide, since patrols didn't come to the planet. Sweet still protested being under APU governance, since the planet had been formed after the fact. Discussions were ongoing, since parliament never did anything the easy way.

"Sounds perfect. What next?"

Lee clapped a hand on her shoulder. "Next, we go over the outline to the parliament meeting chambers again. You really need to stay one hundred percent focused. Gina, pull up the schematics."

The visual that displayed was a mirror image of the halls she'd roamed as a child during parliament sessions. "How did you get this?"

Gina's light blinked. "I hacked their system based on the passcodes and information you gave me."

Of course. The ship could hack anything, it seemed—Sampson had made sure of that. "Ingenious." That was the best Loyda could offer, besides *highly illegal*. She pulled at a loose thread of the sweater she wore. A parting gift Al had given her. He'd said it'd always been hers. *'Even if I gave it to my sister.'*

The bastard didn't seem to get that her goal and purpose was to do something for the greater good. That acting for the benefit of others was far more rewarding then acting for the benefit of oneself.

"Loyda, seriously, pay attention."

She snapped her attention back to the screen, ignoring Lee's frustrated gaze. "The entrance suggestion I made last time is still the best. Minimal guards. The shift changes every six solar hours to reduce exhaustion."

"Lazy bastards," Lee said as she flipped a knife between her hands. "Six-hour shifts means people get careless. Stupid."

"Long shifts do the same thing." Loyda had seen it firsthand. That was why they'd moved to the shorter shifter periods with less off time. "We go through the side entrance, bust into the backroom chambers and head up to the main floor through this far side entrance. That will put us right where we need to be and get Sampson access to the main holo-viewer. That's important. If we send Emilio with Sampson, then Toni, you and I can take the rest of it. Leave Doc and Dottie to guard Gina."

"I don't need guarding." Gina's light went red. It seemed the AI had a personality function that didn't do it any favors.

Sampson shushed her. "She's not implying you can't take care of yourself, but the technology on Saturn is far superior than other planets we have been too. Precautions are a good thing."

Loyda wished she'd told her heart the same thing. Precautions would have been good, but she'd charged forward. And Al, he kept moving in the opposite direction. His whole line and bullshit about how he wasn't any good, how he needed to worry about himself and not others... He'd acted for the benefit of others all the time, but fear had made her believe he'd turned her in. Fear that he resented her living and Frankie dying. This thing between them had been too new, too fresh, and she'd shoved it towards the sun, attempting to root it out.

"We doing okay in here?" Toni's voice filtered in from the doorway.

Al's sister walked into the room with a different hairstyle from yesterday's. Toni kept things fresh by constantly changing her hair and appearance. At first, Loyda had thought the practice silly. Why waste time and effort on something that didn't matter? In the grand scheme of things, this was exactly why Loyda had never fitted in on the uppers. She cared more about people, about life, than what she wore or looked like.

"Yeah, reviewing the plan again because Lee isn't comfortable with it."

Lee scowled. "No, we are reviewing it again because people miss things. You think it's one way and the next time you remember something new. It's just the way minds work. I don't like to operate something without reviewing it a few times."

Sure, that was what the assassin said, but Loyda couldn't help but feel she was being measured to see if her story held up, with the amount of subtle distrust ever-present. It seemed no ship and no crew in the solar system believed in taking someone at their word.

"How about everyone take a break? Sweet said there's a fantastic meal whipped up in the main kitchen."

Akono Sweet's planet of the future had proven a nice haven, though that would change if the APU had their way. Sweet had embraced Emilio's crew with open arms and had been surprised to see Loyda, but had still welcomed her. *Shocking.* She'd fully expected Sweet to object to her presence here.

Sampson jumped towards the door. "I'll be back in a bit. That cook they got here is something else." They didn't have to tell the lanky young man twice. Lee followed only because Loyda saw the look Toni gave the woman.

Loyda hung back, knowing damn well this was a chance for the two of them to have a heart-to-heart. "Listen, I get it. The plan is the most solid, but it will have to—"

"I'm not here to talk about the plan. I believe you know what you're doing, and what you don't know,

Lee can cover. She's broken in to places I could only dream of seeing."

Loyda dragged her foot on the floor. The damn thing was smooth. Smoother than most floors. "Then what do you want?"

"To see how you're holding up. Comments on ship are that you're having trouble sleeping, restless, and maybe missing my troublesome brother."

She sure knew how to put the pin in the firing mechanism.

"I don't miss him."

"You're as bad a liar as my brother is. You got tells just like he does. The way you start playing with the floor with your feet...you get fidgety. I'm surprised he didn't pick up on that."

"He's not a good man. Not a hero." Loyda was hauling out the same tired lines he'd delivered to her.

"Yeah, and you aren't the first person to fall for the bad boy. Emilio is the last person I should have been with, a drug and shine runner paired up with me, an alcoholic. We were a recipe for disaster, but working together, we found reasons to become better people."

Loyda laughed, a sour feel stealing over her stomach. "I can't change him, make him want to be a better person. That comes from inside someone. Besides, my future, my profession, is everything he isn't. I'm on the right side of the law, and how would it look, me being with a habitual liar?"

Toni pointed a finger in her direction. "Yet you can tell when he's lying, can't you? I also noticed he seems to be more honest with you. Well, except for that part where he said he didn't care about you. His hands were twitching hard — surprised you didn't catch that."

Oh, she had, but had ignored it. Why force him to fight for something if he wouldn't do it himself? There were lines she had to draw in the sand, boundaries to place for both their sakes. "He walked away."

"Did you mention that you loved him and needed him? Because people typically like knowing when others care about them. Or at least it helps the decision-making process."

"Why should I put my heart on the line? He proved everything by walking away, by leaving." Loyda crossed her arms, leaning against the table.

"So, you're scared." Toni's smile made Loyda want to punch, kick and scream, because that scared feeling of rejection, of being wanted for any other reason besides just loving her, clawed at her insides.

"Yes! I'm scared shitless. He could try to use me, just like my dumb fiancé did. What about his own agenda? What if he forces himself to stop using his tells? There's too much risk, and I can't give this up for him. Should I give everything up for him?"

Toni shook her head and reached out, clasping one of Loyda's hands between her own. "No, you shouldn't diminish yourself or your efforts for him. He should respect you enough to know you have to end this. You're going to influence the future, change things. I know that much, based on what you are doing. But once you're done, maybe my brother isn't something you'll have to give up."

Loyda nodded, letting the thought buoy her. An additional ray of hope for what she was fighting for. A future where she could be with who she wanted.

* * * *

Al grabbed a socket wrench. "I'll get you locked in place, ya devil."

The old ship in front of him, up on mounters to keep it steady, was his parents'. A vessel they'd once used for short travel distances to and from the moon. Something that, with enough work, could get him back to Callisto station to get his flash, and eventually to his final retirement spot. But none of that would be possible if he didn't get the damn thing working, a pain in the ass the old freighter, with fried circuits, a busted front end and a slip drive and computer older than he was.

"Well, I see you're keeping yourself distracted. I get it—still pissed they took your ship." His mother's voice—not too sharp, not too nice either. She always let her words speak harsh truths with as little tact as possible. But at her core she meant well. At least Al had believed that for the most part, with him.

"I hope to get this working."

She patted him on the shoulder, and he leaned up from the ship's engine to look her in the eye. "It would be nice, but's not a requirement. We need to talk about other things."

More than a year prior, Al's father had been killed by his sister's right hand and best friend, Lee. Bad situation, that, but Al knew his father, knew the older Smith patriarch would have never laid down his weapon without firing or being fired upon. That was why Toni had taken off as soon as she'd dropped Al on Mars. His sister and mother still weren't speaking. *Not my problem to solve.*

A crappy situation all around. His mother wanted revenge. Al wanted to move on.

Now…she wanted Al to take over.

"I already told you, Mom. I'm not staying." Normally he would have lied, pacified her and snuck off with the ship. That was what he'd done the last time he'd left home. *Running away on a body collector barge in search of a better life.* Too bad he hadn't found it. But something inside, ever since he'd left Loyda, had broken. Lying seemed pointless—he was too old to be hiding from his responsibilities, from what he wanted in life.

"But it would be easy. You said they aren't after you for leaving, ending the commission early. Get what you need from wherever and take over. There are so many holes to fill since your father was taken from us."

Al tried to stop himself from snorting and failed.

"Don't act like that, Alexander Smith. Your father was taken from us."

"Whatever you have to tell yourself, Mom. I won't stop your grieving process." He was grieving too. The loss of the woman who wouldn't give up her damn mission to save the universe. A one-woman army, dragging his sister into some sort of mess. Except he wasn't a saver. Nope, lying and thieving were what he did, had done and his mother wanted him back in the fold to do it again. *Nope, never again.* Because it wasn't worth it.

"I got a lot of work to do."

His mother dragged over a stool and sat down on it. Bebe Smith had bright bleach-blonde hair and an affinity for cigars. She lit one now and took a long drag. After the breath, she smiled. "And you were always good at multi-tasking. Tell me what happened. You're not the same Al Smith, rough-housing tumbler, eager for a fight and teller of tall tales. I'll admit I haven't heard one of your stories in a while."

Fine – she wants a story, I'll give her one.

"I picked up a new processer and it turned out she was trouble. Got on the wrong side of the law and fell in love."

"Shortest story I ever heard. How is the law involved?"

Al sighed and went back to wrenching, loosening the sockets holding together the crappy slip drive. "The processer was the law. Prettiest woman I'd ever met, couldn't refuse her, couldn't walk away. Turned out to be a damn pup investigator. I fell in love with the very type of person you and Dad always told me not to. You both always said such a union would never work."

Dearest Bebe laughed. She straight out laughed so hard she choked on a bit of smoke. Al didn't move to help. His mother wouldn't want it. She liked to figure things out all by herself. "Why wouldn't it work? Because you have different ideals? And what's wrong with fighting for the people you love, dearest boy?"

He stopped wrenching and almost tossed the wrench down. Instead he closed his eyes, searching for clarity. "You're not making sense."

"Oh, let me clear that up then. I told your father the day you were born you'd do great things, you'd be someone better than us, more than us. Sounds to me like this woman could inspire you to do just that. To influence the future of all the planets and moons, and not by lying or manipulating, but through love. Nothing is greater than that."

Damn if his mother didn't contradict with a couple of sentences everything she'd taught him over the years of his childhood. It was crap.

"So, you'd support a union between me and a pup investigator." He eyed her from the side, eager to gauge her reaction.

"I'm not saying I'd be thrilled at the idea of you being connected to the law or being far away from home, but I would never tell you to deny love."

"What if she rejects me?"

Bebe laughed. "Then she's a damn fool and doesn't deserve you."

Al nodded and removed the last bolt. He lifted the slip drive out and dropped it to the floor.

"Still amazes me how big you got, how strong. It would normally take two or three men to lift those out."

"I'm special."

"Yes, you are," Bebe leaned up on her tiptoes and Al leaned down so his mother could kiss him on the cheek.

"Hey, Al!" This from one of the Smith lackeys at the ship hangar door.

"You got my attention."

"You have a visitor. Tuatha Anu."

Chapter Twenty-One

Before they departed Eden, Sweet made Loyda promise she'd return. She agreed because it was the polite thing to do, but everyone was aware that the future remained uncertain. Anything could happen between now and when they landed on Saturn. Never mind the fact that the ambassadors and parliament could still rule in favor of Tuatha. Loyda shuddered at the idea of giving up her life and changing nothing.

"This can't be for nothing."

Emilio coughed, making her aware of his presence. "I agree. What happens if we can't make them listen, if they won't see reason?"

Loyda looked away from her view of space, out of the side window on the ship's bridge. "You get Toni, your crew and Gina the hell out of there and never look back. Don't stick around and attempt to rescue someone unable to be saved."

"So, you're a self-sacrificer. I can respect that, though it goes against my instincts. This crew, these people, are my family. If what my wife says about Al's feelings for you is true, that makes you family too."

Now Loyda understood how secrets couldn't be kept on a ship—even on a different one, every inch of her business was supplied to other members. Loyda didn't look at him, refusing to give anything else away. "I appreciate the gesture and effort, but really, one life isn't worth it when many can be saved."

"How many do you save if you die? None that I know of."

Those words haunted Loyda for the next two days as she rehashed the plan and finalized the video feed. They all agreed it was better to broadcast her information than put her in the parliament chamber. No matter what Loyda said, the crew of *Gina* couldn't stand the idea that she would put herself in harm's way. Lee called her an easy target. Sampson said it was silly when he could rig up something equally effective. Doc told her not to be crazy and Dottie just said that she understood Loyda's perspective. Dottie was from the uppers, if her speech patterns were any indication, though Loyda never had time to ask.

On the third day, they passed Jupiter. Loyda had started writing letters to her parents, to Al…she needed to put her emotions into words, if those things wouldn't be said in person. She'd finished confessing her love, a love born from physical attraction, then admiration for the battles Al had fought, for himself and her. That was when Gina's light blinked.

"Loyda, I am being intercepted by an APU Class A cruiser. Unfortunately, I am no match for this type of ship. They are hailing and want to speak with you. If you don't speak to them, they will blow me out of space. Though it's physically impossible to blow me out of space… maybe around it—"

"Gina, tell them I'll be there momentarily. Are Toni and Emilio aware?"

"Yes, they are. Waiting for you on the bridge now."

Loyda stood and straightened her sweater, the same one Al had given her. She couldn't take it off, and the damn thing warmed her like nothing else. She pulled her hair back and up into a half knot and secured it with the writing stick she'd been using.

Grav boots on, she marched for the bridge with new resolve. She'd expected this, to get caught before they reached the destination. She was prepared to convince the ship's captain to let them pass, as she was on her way to Saturn for the tribunal.

Those words hovered on her lips as she entered the bridge, coming to a stop next to Toni and Emilio, facing the holo-screen. A weathered, grizzled older man looked down at her. She took a deep breath, "Captain, I am Loyda Miles and I am here to inform you that—"

"Get out of my way. I will speak with her." The older man was shoved out of the way by a smaller woman, a woman with short wild blonde hair and glasses. "Ah, Loyda Miles. We meet in person at last. I thought you'd be a redhead."

"And I thought you would be..."

"Less frazzled, dazzled, I know. It's hell traveling on an APU cruiser instead of my own vessel, but desperate times and all that. Afraid I don't pack my best attire or all the fancy details when I'm on a mission to track down a ruthless killer."

Her hands were widely gesticulating, her body swaying. If Loyda hadn't known better, she'd guess the evil Tuatha had some sort of shine or drug addiction. But more than likely it was part of an act. An act to make her seem less threatening, which Loyda didn't buy, especially with the off-hand, outrageous comments.

"I'm not a killer."

"That's up for debate at the moment, but anything can be negotiated, wouldn't you agree?"

There were no words from Emilio or Toni, or anyone else for that matter. Loyda was on her own. "I'm willing to listen to what you have to say."

"Don't listen to me. Listen to the voice of reason from the man who loves you."

Her heart stuttered against her ribcage, a dumb organ eager to see Al appear on the screen. *Holy hells, if she's captured Al...* Instead, Gaylord appeared and the pressure building in her blood evaporated away. The betraying bastard was the last person she wanted to see.

"Loyda, darling. I told you I wouldn't give up. I'm not, by the way, and Tuatha is willing to get rid of everything if you just turn over whatever data or information you have and come willingly."

She scoffed. "Unbelievable. You believe her words over mine, the woman you want to be married to the rest of your life?"

"I didn't say that. I just said we need to quit while ahead. There's a reason for all Tuatha's efforts. Is it really our place to challenge existing members of parliament on their policies and projects? The whole of the ambassadors can make that decision without our meddling."

The words were like oil to a fire. Loyda clenched her fists and stomped a foot twice. She needed to punch something. Toni reached out, wrapped a hand around her fist and squeezed gently.

"People are dead. Mothers, brothers, sisters, children…all dead because of her. I can't stand by and allow that to continue."

"But it won't."

Loyda laughed out loud, bold and strong. "You are disgrace, Gaylord. Tuatha, try again. I don't believe a word this one says, and if he thinks I'm marrying him or that he's getting my mother's seat in parliament, he's delusional."

Tuatha appeared once more, shoving Gaylord offscreen. Loyda enjoyed the little yelp and subsequent crash which she hoped was her ex-fiancé.

"Fine, you need more convincing. I'll agree I didn't know what you or your parents saw in that fop Gaylord. He's not exactly the brightest, strongest candidate for an ambassador role. Easily bought. Why don't you listen to your parents instead?"

Tuatha motioned to someone out of view, and the next thing Loyda saw were her parents being escorted in front of the screen. Her father looked less than thrilled and her mother a bit fearful, pulling at the edges of her knitted shawl. Loyda had been annoyed before, but the fear came back anew. Tuatha had her parents. How many more people was the woman hiding on that cruiser in an attempt to force Loyda's compliance?

"Daughter, we ask that you give up whatever foolhardy plan you have. Nothing can prevent a tribunal at this point. Your running stunt made the resolve even greater. Give up and Tuatha has agreed to help you, to help bring the ambassadors to our side of things."

Her mother nodded at her father's words before taking over. "Yes, it's a big political game. Let that game be played and honored. We can help. Tuatha and her husband can assist."

It was as though she'd stepped into some alternate reality, hearing her parents say words that she'd never dreamed they would. *Politics, a game...* Her parents took their roles and positions as sacred duties and had trained her to believe the same, though she wasn't the best person to be an ambassador. She wouldn't take bribes or be corrupted. To hear them admit such a thing made her question the sincerity of their plea. Then her mother winked, and Loyda wouldn't give up. *No matter what.*

"These words mean nothing to me, Tuatha. Bringing you down is worth far more."

Her parents disappeared and Loyda prayed silently to the goddess for protection, to keep her parents from harm until they could rescue them.

"Fine, so none of this appeals to you. Inspector Miles, you drive a hard bargain. What if I told you I have the perfect alternative, a replacement person who's willing to confess to the crimes you're accused of? All you have to do is give me all the data you collected."

* * * *

Al wanted to tell Loyda no, to yell at her to stick to her guns, but there were more lives on the line than just his. His sister's, her parents'. The only reason he was willing to do what Tuatha said was because he'd decided he'd do whatever he could for Loyda. He'd said he would be Tuatha's scapegoat, but she'd changed the damn rules.

She wanted his debt to her paid in full, or so she said. Leaving him on Mars until it was time to face a tribunal was unacceptable. Locking him up and dragging him on the hunt for Loyda had made much more sense. In the days that had followed, he'd gotten to see her take control of Loyda's parents, threaten them...and that was what had gotten him beat up.

"She took the bargain. I'm surprised. She must really love you," Tuatha commented before she tweaked his nose, sending a spasm of pain lighting up the nerves in his face.

Al growled. "Love for me doesn't factor in. There are more lives on the line, more at stake. I'm just a means to an end."

"I'm not so sure. She seemed pained to see you all messed up. Now, I'm glad you wanted to try and fight back. My guards were a surprising match for you too. Especially since you're larger than them."

Her guards were part of an elite trained team of assassins, the same group Lee had defected from several years prior. So no matter how big he was, his rudimentary bar-scrapping fighting style held no candle to what those bastards were capable of.

"I think they could beat a giant." The assassins in question, the pair of them, grabbed him by the arms and he walked willingly out of the bridge to the ship and down a side hallway, to the galley. There he took a seat next to Loyda's mother.

She looked like she hadn't slept in a solar week, the same as Loyda's father. Al hadn't caught their names, but that didn't really matter. Not when he was determined to ensure they stayed unharmed.

Tuatha tapped the main table with one finger. "Well, ambassadors, your daughter turns out to be not as selfish as I feared. She's agreed to give me the information she has. Al has graciously also agreed to confess to her crimes. I get what I want, and you get your daughter back."

Gaylord made some sort of weird throat noise. "Yes, but is she still innocent or tainted by this heathen from Mars?"

"Oh, I tainted her, every possible position… direction… You get my seconds, Gaylord, if she'll let you touch her. Rumor is no man can satisfy a woman I've had."

"Why, you Mars son of a whore—"

Tuatha laughed. "Ooh, I wonder if that's true. We might have time before Loyda arrives to test out your theory, Smith."

Al almost gagged but swallowed his inclination. He needed to appear tough for this moment. "It holds some truth if it's making Gaylord angry. He can't stand the idea of being inadequate, though that's all he'll ever be."

A table separated them, half as wide as Al's height. Yet Gaylord screamed in frustration and tried to launch himself across it. "How dare you!"

A snap of Tuatha's fingers and that pair of assassins had moved away from Al and gone to grab Gaylord.

"Disgrace," Loyda's father muttered.

"Agreed. You are a child, Gaylord. I would never give my family seat to one who acts like you. Have dignity. Respect the fact that my daughter would still choose you at all, though I would dissuade her of the notion, first chance I got to speak with her," Loyda's mother added.

Al liked these two. They could all agree that Loyda's one-time fiancé wasn't worth the title anymore. That meant something to him. But he wanted to upset the delicate balance of the crew of this ship even more, and that started with Gaylord being shaken up before

Loyda arrived. "You know we made love under a lit-up starry night sky. Of course, the ship's windows didn't do it justice, and they got all fogged up when I moved her against the glass and drove into her. She thought I might break the ship, the noise she made about it. Though they may have been screams of pleasure, I'm not—"

"Shut up! I can't listen to any more of this." Gaylord stomped towards the entrance, then turned around for dramatic effect. "I'll be there when they kill you. I'll be smiling and clapping the entire time."

Then he was gone, leaving the room and everyone in peace. Al sighed and put his head down against his arms on the table, wary of touching his nose or any part of his sore eye. He wished he could have had a doctor look at it, but Tuatha had refused.

"What made you kill the pilot? Do you love the inspector that much?" Tuatha's questions forced Al to raise his head.

"What are you talking about?"

"Callisto station. I have the video. You killed your pilot—known her since you were kids on Mars, and yet her attempting to shoot our Inspector Miles was enough for you to take her life. Not render her unconscious but end her. Why?"

There wasn't a good answer for that, and Tuatha didn't deserve his truth. He'd give her a portion of it. "I killed her because she wouldn't stop attempting to kill Loyda, and that worked against me. It's always about me, Tuatha. Thought you would have figured that out by now."

Tuatha tapped him on the chin and he did his best to accept it, to not spit in her face or plow his forehead into hers. Those ideas, murderous things, ran rampant in his head, a variety of options, sights, sounds and sensations that he could imagine, that he'd employed on others in the past and wanted to enact on her damn smug face.

"Yes, well, this isn't at all selfish, Big Al." She said his name with a waggle of her eyebrows, the effect making him swallow back bile.

"Isn't it? There'll be books about me, stories to tell. The man who killed an entire ring jail, hell… I talk to the right people and you won't be the savior of humanity and space travel. Alexander Smith of a Mars racing and mining family will be. What a story."

Tuatha's smile melted away into a glowering frown, a reminder of how easily she could flop from all happy sunrays to the deepest of black holes, ready to suck a person dry. His limited interactions with her had taught him this much, but he'd said what he needed to in the hopes she would go away, disappear into the ether and leave him a few moments of peace. Moments that he'd be hard-pressed to get in the future with where he was headed.

"They won't be talking about you at all. Not in history books, nor in private circles. You'll become just the face and name of a fool who tried to dismantle years of hard government work and effort and failed. Failed to get away with your crimes and I, Tuatha Anu, stopped you." The woman slapped him, making sure to hit him in his already bruised eye, then stomped away, out of the room.

"You are not as selfish as you say. Helping our daughter, trying to stay away from that woman… Who knew she was capable of such atrocities, and willing to do whatever, kill whomever to keep them secret?"

Al turned his head a bit, to try to look at Loyda's mother. "This universe is full of people just like her. The only difference is she found a way to get power and keep it. But really, there's no escaping her kind. Those who believe so fiercely in what they're doing at the expense of everyone else."

"Still, you aren't them," her mother said, reaching out and putting a hand to his shoulder. A small gesture of comfort he couldn't afford.

Tuatha's voice echoed outside the room. "Fine, Inspector, I'll show them to you, but this doesn't change our bargain. I want the data immediately after, then you can gather your parents and go on your merry way."

Lies. Tuatha would kill them all. Loyda's mother had confirmed it. The madwoman had to ensure no one survived to speak of her crimes. Al believed they'd fire on Toni's ship if given the chance, and he didn't know how to stop it. None of that mattered when Loyda stepped over the threshold. He experienced instant elation at her presence, looking her over with even one eye, drinking in her appearance. He didn't miss that she was wearing his sweater. The one he'd knitted for his sister, because hers was long gone, lost on the Acheron, a ship he'd never see again.

"Al." She said his name with a touch of breathlessness and rushed to his side.

Her hands connected with his, the bond more than he could have ever asked for. It was narly a week since he'd seen her and it had been too long. Sacrificing their future, his life, for a chance at her having one would have been worth it, though knowing she'd die anyway seemed like a waste of a deal in his mind.

"Loyda, you should have run."

"I agree," said her father. "Running would have made more sense. This is madness."

Tuatha chuckled. "They've always told me I'm a little crazy, but crazy actions yield life-changing results, wouldn't you say?"

Loyda squeezed his hand and he squeezed back. This wasn't going the way they'd planned at all. The way he'd envisioned their brief reunion. The look in Loyda's eyes reminded him of someone who'd accepted their end. A person making a choice that might not end well.

"Which is exactly why you're going to let all of us leave," she said to Tuatha. A matter-of-fact request without a question.

"Why would I do that?"

Loyda pulled up the bottom edge of the sweater. "Because I'm strapped with enough explosive to blow this ship into a million pieces."

Chapter Twenty-Two

Inside, Loyda was the biggest ball of nerves and wreckage. On the surface, she was as cool as a cucumber. She lowered the bottom of the sweater back into place, her threat made. Seeing Al in person, the damage that had been done to him, hurt in a way she hadn't expected. She wanted to kill Tuatha even more now. Being this close to the woman, she could have just reached for her and snapped the devil's neck in half.

It was made all the worse when Tuatha started to laugh, a small thing that turned loud, riotous and echoed through the galley they stood in. "You expect me to believe you'd blow up everyone you hold dear? Just to get me?"

"Yes, because you aren't going to let us go anyway." She needed to stall. Stall for as much time as she could.

Al opened his mouth to say something and she looked at him, really gave him the stare, hoping he got the silent message. *Shut the hell up.*

"True…though I was going to enjoy watching you think I would let you go. Except I still don't believe you."

There was no way to measure if the assigned time had passed. Toni, Emilio, Lee and Sampson were all working their way towards their designated posts. Their madcap crew refused to give up yet, even if the odds were stacked against them. But she wouldn't know if they made it in time.

"You should believe me. I'm a woman with nothing to lose. That's the thing you underestimated, Tuatha. People with nothing to lose are dangerous. People who believe everyone is out to kill them are dangerous too. Maybe you should have thought about that before putting everyone in a room together."

"Yes, but one doesn't go from being a person who fights to bring justice to missing dead people toward killing unnecessarily."

Loyda skirted her finger around the trigger for the bomb strapped to her chest. Dottie and Lee had secured everything. It was real. It would work, both ladies had told her, and she'd been reminded of suicide bombers of old Earth. Men, women and children who'd acted as martyrs in attacks on their enemies. Lord, everything she'd never wanted to be, but would if it saved the rest of the universe from this woman. She'd at least go out with a last look at Al. Though if she acted this situation out correctly, she'd be the exact opposite of a bomber.

The damn man appeared miserable, hunched over his stool. They'd suffered enough.

"Who says this isn't necessary?" she asked. "You'd be surprised what's necessary and how far a person is willing to deviate from their belief system after they've had everything taken from them."

Tuatha scoffed. "Then go ahead. I spent my whole life in hell. I dare you."

"No, you said you wanted to bargain. To make a deal. So talk. Give me a really good reason to not set this off."

"Why talk when the end is so near? You keep fighting for dead people when the damage is done. Turn everything over and I'll make sure the end comes quickly."

Tuatha wasn't even attempting a pretense anymore. Loyda had to continue and she only prayed everyone was in place. She started the countdown button. The beeping made her mother and father jump. Al reached for her, but she moved out of his reach and Tuatha grinned.

"You're as crazy as I am. I love it."

"You won't get away with murdering current ambassadors of parliament," Loyda replied in defiance.

"I can and I already have. You don't rise to the ranks of parliament, the daughter of stoners from the moon, by playing nice. No, I fought for my spot. Jockeyed for position, found myself an ambitious husband, almost as ruthless as I am. Parliament also likes to back visionaries, people with a little more guts and glory than most ambassadors have." With each word, Tuatha attempted to move closer to Loyda, so Loyda started to move too, never letting Tuatha out of her sight or to get too close.

"Guts and glory don't mean murdering people."

"My vision had nothing to do with murder. No, it was all about a new fuel source, metal ore compressed and transformed into a powder more powerful than carbon. The dawn of a new age of space travel. Imagine, Loyda, a world where are ships no longer run on the dust of our own fellow man. Bone powder would be a thing of the past and we could travel farther, faster. Already we see the strain on supply – bigger ships, using more technology, require extra stores. Bone powder supplies dwindle, birth rates are down, people are afraid to give their children the supplements that keep them alive because they could end up giants like your captain here, or with deformities."

The present sounded awful. "So where is the future?"

"It failed," Tuatha replied. Then she shrugged. "Eh, the technology has some flaws and issues I didn't foresee, ones I can't fix. But there's no need for it anymore, because the bone stores of the APU have been replenished, to near maximum capacity, thanks to my genius idea of killing the filth on Callisto and raiding the Saturn ring jail. With proper rationing, we wouldn't need another culling for at least a decade."

Culling…goddess. "We're not animals created for the slaughter."

"But aren't we? The solution isn't ideal, though I'm proud to say I've brought about this momentous occasion. I'm saving the precious future of the detective agency – those men and women can do their jobs in the future. The same for space travel, legitimate merchants and countless others."

The steady droning beep coming from the bomb on her chest was the only sound in the room. Al and her parents wore a mixture of emotions, from seething anger to disgust. Her mother cried, though. She'd instilled the sense of right and wrong Loyda had carried with her since childhood and she'd always believed strongly in protecting those she'd been appointed to serve, thought it appeared she was aware of how they'd been let down.

"So, you'd kill those people again?" *Once more, you dumb bitch. With feeling.*

"Yes! I'd kill them all, whatever it took to maintain my position. Failure would only have yielded poverty. I will be a hero. Now turn the damn bomb off."

Loyda tapped on the bomb and Tuatha jumped.

"Scared?" Loyda asked. "Because you should be. This isn't a bomb. It's a broadcasting device that my friends have been transmitting every word and image on to any open channel system as far as the signal will travel. Kiss goodbye to that hero's welcome."

Tuatha grabbed her hair with both hands and screamed. A bloodcurdling holler that had Loyda scrambling for a weapon. *Anything, even a plate at this point.* The smaller woman charged her, slamming Loyda into the table. Al yelled, but a glance showed him engaged in his own battle with Tuatha's personal bodyguard. They were in trouble. *Where the hell are Toni and Lee?*

Loyda wrestled with Tuatha, which was a bit difficult to do with a broadcasting video device strapped to her chest, but she somehow got her knees up between their bodies, then her feet, and was able to push Tuatha off her. Loyda scrambled to her feet, ripping the sweater off and shredding the fake bomb from her chest and onto the floor. Armed in nothing but a T-shirt separating her bare skin from cold air, she found her parents huddled in a corner, with Tuatha nowhere to be seen.

"You have to head for the docking bay. There's a shuttle there. Get on it, take off and don't look back."

Her mother shook her head. "No, we can't leave you. Too many lives have already been lost."

She looked around, nervous and wanting to find Tuatha. The woman was too damn dangerous.

Grabbing her mother in a brief hug, she whispered, "That's why you need to run. You need to tell the story of what happened here. If nothing else, you can be the voice that can confirm what was broadcast today."

Loyda's father leaned into the hug. "You are the bravest woman I've ever known."

"Thank you." Those were the words she'd been aching to hear all her life and now, when they were fighting for their lives, he said them. Then Tuatha appeared again, this time with a gun.

"Mom, Dad, you have to go." Loyda didn't wait for a response. She rose and headed in the direction Tuatha had marched.

Al stood over one of the guards, slamming his head against the floor. Goddess bless, there was blood on his hands, on the floor, but it didn't appear to be his. Tuatha had her gun trained on Al. Loyda sprinted for him, throwing herself through the air, sliding across the big table. Then the shot fired.

The hit hurt. Damn, it hurt and she yelled, falling off the table and right into Al, who gathered her in his arms. "Loyda, you idiot. Why did you do that?"

Loyda moaned. "I saved you. Looks like you're not the only one who can save a life in the universe."

Her eyes got heavy and she just wanted to rest, the ringing in her ears relentless.

"Loyda, stay awake. Loyda!"

Al gently laid Loyda on the floor and looked up. Tuatha stood not too far away, the gun aimed at him.

"Looks like I hit something. Not my intended target, but she'll do."

His vision turned red and he roared, clambering to his feet and stalking toward the woman. The ice-cold bitch stared him down, the nuggets on this murderer unreal. Then she tried to pull the trigger, but the gun misfired and he had his chance.

He wrapped his hand around her throat first then lifted, enjoying her futile attempt to struggle in his hold. The swinging of her legs—he didn't even feel pain each time her feet kicked against his thighs. There was something broken in him, and if Loyda died, it would be gone forever.

"Al, stop! We can't," said Toni, who'd miraculously materialized beside him.

"I would think there are hundreds of reasons why I can. Maybe thousands."

Toni put a hand on his arm, the same arm connected to the same hand holding Tuatha by the throat, at his mercy.

"Loyda needs help. Immediately. Let Emilio and me get this bitch locked up. We need to clear Loyda's name and ensure this woman pays for every life the right way."

Al's chuckle was half-hearted and sour. "Never took you for a right-way type of person, Toni. Besides, what's more fighting then killing her here and letting her become the powder she was so eager to create?"

Tuatha struggled more, fear present in her gaze.

Al dragged her closer, narrowing the distance between their faces. "Oh, yes. You're going to die. Either by my hand or someone else's."

"Al…"

"I killed Frankie for trying to kill the woman I love. I can kill this one too."

Toni sighed. "Lee, he won't listen."

"Al," Lee said. "I'll shoot you in the kneecap if you don't drop her."

Oh, a kneecap would be a small price to pay to see this bitch lifeless on the floor. "I'd accept it."

"Think of Loyda's purpose here. The male-protective shit doesn't serve her or what she needs."

Toni's words, however annoying they were, made sense. And against his better judgment, he let Tuatha drop to the floor. Her gasps of air were the only satisfaction he'd get. Dropping her got the initial shock to wear off and he remembered Loyda. He rushed to her side and picked her up.

She didn't make a noise and he feared the worst, except he could still feel a faint heartbeat.

"Toni, I'll send another shuttle back for you. I'm stealing yours."

Chapter Twenty-Three

Getting to the shuttle wasn't difficult. No one cared who he was or where he was going. With Tuatha caged and her goons dead, everyone else around the ship seemed to wonder what they hell they were supposed to do. People hustled to who knew where. When he reached the shuttle, that was when things got a little crazy, because Loyda's parents were there and immediately concerned about their daughter.

Al ignored their frantic questions. "Hey! Listen up. Can either of you pilot this shuttle?"

Loyda's father nodded. "Yes. I can."

"Then get us the hell out of here. Autopilot should take you to my sister's ship, *Gina*."

They all got seated, but Al refused to put Loyda down.

"We could lay her on the bunk," her mother suggested.

Al shook his head. No way would he put her down until they got to *Gina* and in front of Doc. She'd lost enough blood already, and more continued to seep out into his own clothing. "Makes it more difficult to carry her to the medical bay when we get there. I can hold her."

The ride took forever, and all through it, Loyda's mother talked. She talked about how they would clear Loyda's name, how everyone would know how brave her daughter had been in the face of a madwoman. The words made it sound as if the woman Al loved was not going to make it, that somehow she'd die.

"Could you please stop talking about her like that?" he asked.

"I don't understand."

Al could feel her heart, her shallow breaths. "She's not dead, and she's not dying. Quit talking about her like she it. We just have to get to the doctor."

"We're docking now," announced Loyda's father. He still didn't know or remember their names. Nor did he care.

As soon as the shuttle door aligned and the clicks sounded, followed by the beeping signaling that the pressure seal was made, Al stood. He hated to hear Loyda groan in pain at his effort. Then he headed for the hatch. It opened before he got there.

"Gina, get Doc to the med bay—we need help. Loyda needs help immediately."

Gina's blue light blinked. "He's already been alerted and has asked for you to tell me where she was shot."

"Somewhere in the abdomen or chest. There's too much blood to tell. But she's breathing and her heart is beating."

"Hurry, Al." Gina's parting words scared him, lit the fear of the sun into him. His pace quickened as he rounded the belly of the ship and was finally through the doors of the med bay.

"Put her here," Doc said, pointing at the surgical table in the middle of the room. He was already in protective gear and ready with shears to cut away her clothes. "Are you okay to be present for this?"

Al laid her down as gently as he could, wiping away hair that had fallen into her face, a face far paler than how she usually looked. "I'm fine. I've seen plenty of wounds, had people die in front of me."

"Well, she's not going to die, son. Not if I can help it," the old man replied. Then he got to work, cutting away her shirt—a threadbare thing—and her bra with it. Blood obscured her skin. Doc washed it away, searching for the wound.

When he found it, he placed a hot rod against it and seared it shut. The smell was putrid, but nothing Al hadn't lived through every day as a body collector. Burning flesh meant a full belly and crinkle in hand. In this case, it meant Loyda would bear another scar.

He'd kill anyone who tried to give her another one. From this moment on, he wasn't leaving her sight. Somehow, they would be together.

"Wounds sealed. Cleaned her up, but Al…she's lost a lot of blood," Doc said as he continued wiping away the red liquid from Loyda's skin.

"Spit it out. What does she need?" Al picked up her hand and squeezed it gently.

"A transfusion. Without one, there's nothing we can do for her, and the nearest med stop, no one here has credentials for. Her pulse is very weak."

Al reached up, grabbed the sleeve of his thermal sweater and yanked, pulling the damn thing off in one tug. "Drain me. I don't care. Just save her."

Doc shook his head but went about his business, muttering the entire time. Something about diseases and lack of testing.

"We don't have time for that," Al replied.

Doc grabbed the needle kit, sterilized everything and started working on Al's arm for a vein. "Yeah, I know. Still doesn't make me less skeptical or concerned. A medical professional should always be worried about the health of their patients."

"She's gonna die if we don't do this. You said it yourself."

The needle went in and stung for a split second, then the blood flowed. Al was big—a ton of liquid life flowed in his veins, and for all he knew, he was clean according to his yearly required physical.

Doc hooked everything up and got the blood transferring to Loyda. "Okay, sit back and relax. This will take a while. We have to give her at least two units. Then we'll check her pulse. If needed, we give her two more."

Al nodded his understanding and glanced around. "Can't really sit back without a chair, Doc."

"I'll go get you one." The older man left the room and Al grabbed a sheet and blanket from under the table, covering Loyda up as best he could one-handed.

"Gina, what's the status on the other vessel?"

Blue light flashed through the room. "The vessel has left the area, reporting back to APU outpost on Jupiter. The ambassadors have contacted parliament and demanded a full session within a week. Pursuit of Loyda has ceased and everyone is almost back on ship. Toni, Lee, Emilio and Sampson will be docking within the next fifteen solar minutes."

Things were finally going right for a hot minute…until Al heard the unmistakable wind-up of a plasma gun.

"Pull that damn needle out of her arm, Smith." Gaylord's voice echoed in the room.

How the hell did this piece of crap get on Gina? "Afraid I can't do that."

"Yes, you can, or I'll put a hole in your head. No way will your blood taint my future fiancée."

Gina's light went off. "Al, I have alerted Toni and Emilio of the intruder, but can't get a read on his bio-signature to disable him."

Gaylord laughed. "I'm not as dumb as one would think. My body is implanted to block my heat signature, voice recognition and facial software. I can be anywhere, anytime, and no one would know."

"Well, I'm sure that's great for you, Gaylord, but in about five solar minutes, my sister and her husband are going to come running in here and —"

"Gaylord, how did you get on this ship?" The voice of Loyda's mother was unmistakable. Al didn't move — his legs were already getting tired.

"Harshita, I am here to prevent mistakes from happening. Your daughter's hand was promised to me and I intend to keep that promise."

Al chuckled. He couldn't turn to see exactly what Harshita and Gaylord looked like or even where they were at, but he was done with these silly games. For once, telling the truth had never sounded better. "This is getting old, Gaylord. I already told you Loyda and I bonded in physical ways you could only dream of experiencing. As soon as we're done with this transfusion and she wakes up, I'm asking her to marry me."

A stomped foot. "No! She'll never marry you."

Loyda made a noise and Al looked down at her with concern. Nothing else mattered at all except for this woman. *Screw guns and ex-fiancés, mothers and talking ships.* He didn't need a chair, or anything for that matter, if she was going to live. Her eyes opened and she cleared her throat before weakly blurting out, "I'll marry you, Al. Knitting and all."

He pulled her hand to his lips and kissed it. The sound of Gaylord's outrage was music to his ears as Loyda's eyes closed again. *Let her rest.* The transfusion appeared to be doing something.

"Give me that chair," Harshita said. Then there was a clunk, a plop and a clatter.

"Is he out?" Al asked.

"Yes, for now." Harshita's steps grew closer and she rounded the table, giving Al the courtesy of being able to see her as much she could look him in the eye. "It appears we have some talking to do, especially if my daughter is willing to give up everything for you."

* * * *

Loyda groaned at how it still hurt sometimes to just readjust her body in a chair. She'd been up and moving after a week of bed rest, but in a limited capacity. Back on Saturn in her parents' house, she had constant surveillance, assistance and everything she could want, except for one thing… *Al.*

The man who, after her surgery, had declared he'd marry her, hadn't set foot by her side in the last week. He'd gotten her through those first days then cried off, making her wonder if the proposal had been a ruse to piss her ex-fiancé off even more. Her parents hadn't cared to volunteer where he'd gone, and she'd been forbidden to start making calls or trying to work… *They won't let me do a damn thing.*

Returning to Saturn had done more than just give her a peaceful, sterile place to recuperate. She'd also been cleared of any wrongdoing thanks to her broadcast, which had been replayed in front of

Parliament. They'd enjoyed that video, watching their sins unfold, her father had said. There had also been some outcry, especially since her own father had supported Tuatha and Ambassador Anu on multiple measures in years past.

"Miss Loyda?" The maid's timid voice came from the library entrance.

"Yes?"

"You have a visitor who would like to speak with you, if you feel up to it."

Loyda sighed in relief. "Please, goddess bless. Send them in."

She put her book to the side and tried to sit up a little straighter in her chair. Stupid body, stupid muscly flesh. That was what Doc had called it, told her over and over that she should have been dead. One more inch to the left and it would have severed and shut down her liver. No way would that have ended well.

"Need help?"

Her head snapped up at the sound of Al's voice. She greedily absorbed every facet of him. There was a marked difference from the man she'd met on the Acheron. His hair was trimmed and slicked back, along with a cleaned-up, shorted beard and no nose ring, complete with tunic and pants more of the Saturn style of dress.

"I don't need any help, but I would like to know what's up with this? Trading in thermal sweaters for fancy duds? The reward for bringing in Gaylord and Tuatha Anu must have been a pretty hefty amount of flash."

Al smiled and shook his head. "You always think the worst of me. This" — he motioned to his body, sweeping his arm up and down — "is all attire befitting my recent acceptance of a new job."

"A job doing what?" Her heart fluttered at the possibilities, the implications. To see Al in this type of dress? She'd never expected it, but he looked mouthwatering, and yet she'd been deprived of his presence for over a week.

"An ambassador to parliament. Your father has decided to retire in the wake of the scandal with Tuatha and her husband. He has named me his successor."

Her heart soared, elation rushing through every part of her body. Except… "You don't care about parliament and politics, doing the right thing and stuff."

He shrugged. "Maybe it's time people could rely on me. I guess for all my beliefs in watching out for oneself, I abandoned people when maybe a helping hand would have changed their own courses. Seeing you almost die, watching Tuatha and Gaylord almost get away with this crap—it woke me up. I want to change the system. Your father also did some convincing. He makes a good point that a great way to change things is to inject a different perspective. At least he sold it that way to parliament and they accepted."

Those words sounded exactly like her father, and she wanted to believe in this, what this decision meant. "So that's where you've been?"

"Yep," Al sat down in a chair across from hers, leaning back into the plush brocade. It was like looking at a different person. "Joaquin is a great mentor. I can see where you got so many of your ideas and your sense of duty. He's been showing me the ropes, getting me familiar with the rules, laws and the political game. It's almost as bad as navigating racing politics on Mars."

She smiled, and Al looked away, out of the window, over the spread-out park of the Miles household. There was a little pond with a fountain in the center. The entire scene gave her such peace. Sharing this moment of quiet with him made it more poignant, because she'd never thought it would be possible to make her dreams come true. To have him here.

Al looked back at her and she opened her mouth to speak, to tell him all the feelings building inside her. Except he held up a finger. "Give me just a couple more minutes to get this out. I'm nervous."

She'd never known Al to be nervous. "Okay."

"While your dad's direction is great, I'd feel more comfortable if I had someone else by my side walking me through the process. Someone I admire, who's incredibly beautiful and smart…and someone I love."

Al stood and removed something from his pants pocket, then got down on one knee. The scene was like something out of her wildest dreams. Here in her family home, one of her most favorite of places, with Al holding out her grandmother's wedding ring. "Loyda Miles, will you bind yourself to me in marriage?"

She grinned wildly, tears flowing freely down her face, and she swiped at them with the back of her hand. "It's beautiful, Al, but I'm not sure."

Al's look of happiness faded and Loyda cracked her knuckles.

"You're lying," he said.

"Maybe I am."

He got down on both knees and crawled forward, crowding her space and eliminating any chance of her attempting to escape. But she didn't want to. As he carefully wrapped her up in his arms, she reveled in his strength, his tenderness, then his lips were less than an inch away.

"Marry me, Loyda. Break me in the best of ways."

"Always and forever."

Then he kissed her.

Want to see more like this?
Here's a taster for you to enjoy!

Honey Moon
Arlene Webb

Excerpt

May 5, 2310
Seattle, WA, USA, United Earth

His vision assaulted with vibrancy of dress — shapes and color — Sam worked his long frame down the walkway teeming with humanity. Agoraphobia not his deal, the occasional step on his heel or elbow to the side was nothing to raise blood pressure over. He loved to watch faces, more often seeing beauty and grace instead of conformity and ugliness. Young and old voices jabbered — talking into the wireless connection bubbled about their mouths and directly streaming to their wrist phones — while face-spacing with either an intimate, mini-hologram projection or going pictureless to chatter into the thin, congested air.

"Sorry, ma'am."

"Hey, watch it."

"Asshole. Move along."

"Yeah, baby, grab hold. I'm — wait, no — thief! Stop her!"

The most furious voice drew Sam's attention. The man ahead came to a halt, jarring the foot traffic moving toward the malls and the train lines, to stare at his arm. His bare arm. No wrist phone. The woman a few steps behind the victim stopped as well. Snarling at the people jostling on by with apathetic disrespect for the worldwide Good Samaritan code, she used her phone to snap pics of the young woman attempting to blend in with the group branching away from the shopping center toward the bullet trains.

Sam sighed and eased around an elderly couple to follow after the thief. People were ignorant and desperate. The vast criminal underbelly would snatch up a wrist phone, yes. But the thief would be lucky to get a week's rent in a cubicle shelter and maybe a couple of meals.

Odds were the woman who'd used one hand to grope a man, distracting him so she could slice the phone from his arm and hustle out of his reach, would be ID'd and tracked down within minutes of her picture pinging into World Security. Was stealing such a personal item worth five to twenty years behind bars?

Sam mentally shrugged. Based on the fact the victim still had two hands, at least the thief either hadn't used the latest switchblade to hit the streets or she was damn good. Micro-thin, the blade—known as the diamond-killer—could hide in the palm of a hand like an old-fashioned razor blade and cut through standard wristbands as if pliable metals were tissue paper.

He instinctively tucked his arm closer to his side, hand shoved in his pocket, and glanced at his own wrist phone. Made from inexpensive aluminum alloys processed under super high-pressure torsion, it was strong and incredibly lightweight but vulnerable to the latest weapons. It took a precise and controlled criminal to wield the diamond-killer, withdraw after just a nick through the band, kissing the skin to leave beads of blood but before the weapon chomped through muscle and bone. Hence the range of severity of penalty in this day and age of not if, but when, the perp was caught.

No matter the evolution of the human race, it seemed young and stupid remained constant. Too bad he, despite being in his mid-thirties, still clung to that juvenile mentality of thinking himself invincible, too clever and savvy to ever have his precious neck land on the chopping block. A terrible attitude when preparing to take on supreme forces that may or may not be evil.

Powerful lobbyists, groups of brilliant minds, rarely confronted the slightest infractions done by those behind the world governments, so what chance had a single idiot? Yet how could he pull someone else into his worries? He really should come up with a diabolical scheme that didn't involve a duo, but time wasn't on his side. If he was going to make a move, he had to stop dithering and set in motion the only idea he'd had to get a handle on his growing paranoia.

But what type of bastard seduces—then risks—the life of an innocent? Assuming he managed to bring a horrendous conspiracy into the light of day, it'd be highly unlikely he'd avoid the bullets the moment the prospective villains—either riding that free rocket ride with him or waiting on the moon—understood that he was the whistleblower.

I don't know what else to do. The deck was stacked one way or another, but with stakes this high, he couldn't live with himself if he didn't at least try. To quote a fictional hero from years past—'The needs of the many outweigh the needs of the few'. Too bad he couldn't respond like a famous Vulcan and give the answer—'or the needs of the one'—meaning it was only his bachelor ass on the line.

I need to find a woman. ASAP. Get down on my knee within the month.

Sam pressed on, angling his way to catch the train to take him to his new, one-room lair. Ten minutes of shallow breaths – glad colognes and perfumes were banned on the trains but geez, did someone really have to eat, say...cabbage soup before they went out in public? He happily disembarked.

His building was slotted in an endless row of the same. Sweat coated him by the time he reached the fourteenth floor. Should have taken an elevator, but at least the stairs belonged to him. Any of the elevators in this skyscraper would be packed worse than ants on a dropped ice cream, and he loved the exercise. He regretted reaching his level, causing yet another excuse to drag his heels on bringing the hunt for a fiancée to a close. He was about to embark on a quest from which there'd be little chance of turning back with his freedom, let alone his heart, intact.

He scanned his wrist phone to unlock the door and entered the eight by ten room. This hop online would most likely turn out to be the most asinine thing he'd ever done. He marched the three steps directly to the com-desk, sat and clicked on the icon linking him to what appeared to be a popular dating site.

Christ, I should have done this a week ago. Over a hundred million hopeful saps like him were trolling Arrow to the Heart in this moment. Eight thousand, one hundred and twelve and counting in his current city. Ever the optimist, he wondered, was it lame to think that maybe, just maybe, if he was honest and opened up, he'd find someone to do more than use? A sweetheart to love and cherish?

Right. Then involve this sweetheart in the nuttiest of conspiracy theories.

His fingers flew, tapping away on the flat desktop monitor. Took him three minutes to open a basic want-to-hook-up account. Two minutes too long, but the server was loaded with dreamers.

Sigh. On to the personality profile. Sam only had to lure someone into saying yes. He wasn't worried about winning the amazing newlywed lottos being offered, looks, money, or even finding instant love with the potential to endure the test of time. That'd be too much to ask. A woman with integrity, compassion and some balls? Not literally, but willing to take a huge risk for the greater good. Surely that was feasible?

Home of Erotic Romance

Sign up for our newsletter and find out about all our romance book releases, eBook sales and promotions, sneak peeks and FREE romance books!

About the Author

Landra Graf consumes at least one book a day, and has always been a sucker for stories where true love conquers all. She believes in the power of the written word, and the joy such words can bring. In between spending time with her family and having book adventures, she writes romance with the goal of giving everyone, fictional or not, their own happily ever after.

Landra loves to hear from readers. You can find her contact information, website details and author profile page at https://www.totallybound.com